POWER
GRIDS
ARE
DOWN

By Brian H Cole

2024

Dedicated to my wife Patti

Copyright 2024

Notes Power Grids Down

Registration Number TXu 2-425-607
Effective Date of Registration: March 26, 2024
Registration Decision Date: March 23, 2024
The title was changed later to Power Grids are Down
Plus

Power Grids are Down

Registration Number TX 9-516-939
Effective Date of Registration: August 12, 2024
Registration Decision Date: July 9, 2025

ISBN-13: 979-8-9876609-6-6

Printed In the United States of America (Amazon)

BOOK PREVIEW

The final day of this year's week-long fishing trip was nearly over, and they all caught more than expected. Brad Zimberman and three of his best friends were settling in for a comfortable evening near the entrance to a calm inlet (fjord) within the Allusion islands. The weather was perfect on this late August day, and they were preparing fish fillets for their final night's dinner before the trip back home.

The evening was comfortable as the sun set and darkness invaded the sky above them, and this is when Brad noticed a strange orange and red glow in the distance. As he pointed it out to the guys, a separate and second glowing object appeared. It didn't take long before a third glowing object appeared, and it was at this time they could tell that the objects were traveling towards them. The objects were coming from Russia and were traveling hyper-fast and low near the water to avoid radar, and that's when Brad yelled, "Missiles!".

The first of the three missiles traveled not more than 100 yards out from the fjord entrance. The second and third missiles followed about one minute apart. Just after the missiles passed their boat, they turned nearly vertical but clearly headed toward the lower 48 States.

Brad knew what these were, and they were missiles armed with nuclear weapons designed to create a ***High-altitude ElectroMagnetic Pulse***, or HEMP for short. They were designed to take out electronics and the power grids.

What happens during and after a HEMP attack, and how do the people of the United States recuperate?

How will Americans struggle for survival after modern life changes in an instant?

INDEX

INTRODUCTION

This book starts with known physics and science and then slow steps into science fiction. This was done to make the book's science fiction part more believable.

Please meet the following people in this novel.

Or

Alternatively, go straight to Chapter 1 and return here later for more information on the characters if needed.

Brad Zimberman – Brad is the main character of this book, and much of this novel revolves around his experiences. He is from Rapid City, South Dakota. He started work out of high school at Blink Construction and worked his way up to a Lineman. After ten years, he took another job with a federal power administration in Gillette, Wyoming. Brad lives with a lady named Ella, and she is his life partner.

Ella – Ella and Brad are an unmarried couple that lives together. Ella is from Rapid City, South Dakota, and went to high school with Brad.

Tim – One of the Dispatch Managers who works for the same federal agency that Brad also works for. Tim and Brad have worked together for many years. They both are dedicated to their work, and always look at ways to improve and protect the power grid.

Troy - CB and Ham radio operator in Canada, and met Brad and his fishing friends when they traveled through Canada from Alaska to the United States. Troy became Brad's trusted friend during the difficult times after the blast.

TJ - CB and Ham radio operator in Gillette, Wyoming. TJ becomes a key person for communications while cell towers are inoperative.

Terry – Terry is one of Brad's biker friends from high school. Terry has lived in Gillette, Wyoming, since graduating high school. The jobs in Gillette pay much better than in Rapid City, so Terry started working in the coal industry. He stayed at the same job his entire career and became well-known in the community. Terry is an avid biker, and he and his wife travel to Sturgis every August.

Wichapi & Hotah – These two people were briefly mentioned at the end of this novel. They were free Lakota Indians when the Pine Ridge Indian Reservation was created. They both became a legend in this area of the country.

Chris - The Lead FBI agent assigned to South Dakota is Chris. He was initially from Rapid City and was comfortable in this area of the country. Chris moved to Denver to get a job as an investigator in Denver. He recently changed jobs to the FBI in Denver, and this was his second assignment in South Dakota as an FBI agent. Chris had a rough start but had the right skills to succeed. He already knew several people in the area from his first FBI job in South Dakota, to include Maka, Chaiton, Ann and Ryan.

Ryan - Ryan grew up in Rapid City, South Dakota, and now lives with his wife, Ann, in Hill City, South Dakota. Ryan never had an education beyond high school and barely made it that far. He worked various jobs to survive and bought a small home in Hill City. Ryan loved to fish and hike in the Black Hills, and he developed a natural skill for mineralogy and structural geology in his search for gold. Ryan didn't get rich with gold, but he considered himself rich by meeting and marrying his soul mate, Ann. Together, they earned more money, and he eventually bought a Harley-Davidson motorcycle. Ryan and Ann loved their new life and became regulars in Sturgis, Deadwood, and other places in the Black Hills. Ryan and Ann became well known as the kind of people to help those who needed help.

Ann - Ann and Ryan are married. Before their marriage, Ann grew up in Rapid Valley, which is a community next to Rapid City, South Dakota. Ann is a beautiful lady with the same hopes and dreams as Ryan. She worked various jobs in Rapid City and Hill City and had a natural gift for sales and marketing. Her marketing ideas helped her career immensely, making her well-respected in Hill City.

Maka - Maka is the sister to Chaiton. She lost her parents to a terrible car accident when she was young. She lived with her relatives in North Rapid and also had a great mentor with a lady named Jennifer (Jen), life partner to Chris (introduced earlier). Maka grew up hard but turned her life around and eventually became a Rapid City police officer.

Chaiton - Chaiton is the brother to Maka. As mentioned above, he lost his parents while he was very young, but with the help of Jen and his relatives, he became a good, responsible man. However, he lived a party lifestyle in high school and hung out with a rough crowd. Although he had some difficulty in high school, he eventually took the lead from his sister and became a Police Officer in Rapid City, but he also maintained friendships with his old high school friends.

CHAPTER 1 – ON A NORMAL DAY

The final day of this year's week-long fishing trip was nearly over, and they all caught more than expected. Brad Zimberman and three of his best friends were settling in for a comfortable evening near the entrance to a calm inlet (fjord) within the Allusion islands. The weather was perfect on this late August day, and they were preparing fish fillets for their final night's dinner before the trip back home. As tradition, they each brought a bottle of their favorite alcohol, and this year's theme brought the best of vodka, given the near proximity to Russia. Brad, however, brought his typical Kentucky bourbon, Woodford Reserve. None of them smoked, but each brought a cigar, as tradition, from the first planned fishing trip over 15 years earlier.

Brad and his friends knew each other from high school and reconnected about 15 years ago after they all found their footing in the workforce. Brad was the only one to leave Rapid City, South Dakota, as a high voltage lineman, and the other three guys found good employment building custom homes in the Black Hills of South Dakota. Brad's job developed into a crew supervisor for the only federal government power department in the western United States. He knew his job well, and part of his success was his exceptional knowledge of Dispatch. Dispatch was located in Gillette, Wyoming, and this office controlled the power grid for most of the western grid, including three converter stations that transferred power between the eastern grid and the western grid. The converter stations transfer power between grids by converting power from AC to DC and then back to AC in the next grid. This conversion was done because the eastern grid was permanently in a different phase than the western grid, and this was the best way to connect the grids to one another. The three converter stations were located in Sidney, Nebraska, and Rapid City, South Dakota, and one was called the Stegall Station, located between Torrington, Wyoming, and Scott's Bluff, Nebraska. All of these stations had two full-time technicians, but none of the stations were manned 24 hours per day. Rather, they had alarms to notify Dispatch of issues, which would, in turn, notify the nearest technician of the issue. This process worked well because each technician could arrive at the station within 15 minutes.

The evening was perfect as the sun set and darkness invaded the sky above them, and this is when Brad noticed a strange orange and red glow in the distance. As he pointed it out to the other guys, a separate and second glowing object appeared. These objects were weird, too weird, so they all grabbed binoculars and their cell phone cameras. It didn't take long before a third glowing object appeared, and it was at this time they could tell that the objects were traveling towards them. The objects were coming from Russia and were traveling hyper-fast and low near the water to avoid radar, and that's when Brad yelled, "Missiles!".

The first of the three missiles traveled not more than 100 yards out from the fjord entrance, so Brad and his friends got some great pictures. The second and third missiles followed about one minute apart. Just after the missiles passed their boat, they turned nearly vertical but clearly heading toward the lower

48 States. Within a minute of the Russian missiles going vertical, the United States defense missile system kicked in a multitude of missiles launching from various island locations all along the Allusion Islands. This defensive action was an incredible sight from their boat in the now darkness. The sun sets late in the day in this area of Alaska, so this all occurred near 10:30 pm local time. Unfortunately, none of the American missiles could catch the hypersonic Russian missiles.

The Department of Defense was now aware of this unprovoked attack and was taking on defensive positions. It didn't take more than 5 minutes for emergency messages to be sent to all US bases worldwide, as well as all naval vessels and other outposts. The United States was somewhat prepared for this type of attack and had been planning for it for years. Brad also knew what was happening and quickly explained to his friends that the missiles were nuclear weapons that would be detonated 100 miles above the United States in an attempt to take out electronics. Electronics included the three main American power grids (Eastern Grid, Western Grid, and Texas Grid). It would also include satellites in line of sight of the explosions. Brad briefly explained what is termed a HEMP or **H**igh-altitude Electro**M**agnetic **P**ulse.

"Theoretically, if a nuclear bomb is exploded, say 100 miles above the Earth, high-intensity particles will be sent out in all directions of the blast. These particles (radiation) can directly affect unprotected satellite electronics, taking the entire satellite out of use. However, radiation can cause much more damage to

Earth *(see References 1, 2, 3, and 4)*. As the particles travel through the Earth's atmosphere, electromagnetic fields are created, sending high-frequency electromagnetic waves (photons) down to Earth. When these electromagnetic photons reach the Earth, they can take out microelectronic devices and, worse yet, the power grid. This damage happens when these super high-frequency electromagnetic photons latch onto conductors for distribution and high-power transmission lines. They then travel down the outside of the conductor at near the speed of light and into electronic components of the power grid, including transformers. These photons, in turn, takes out the most vulnerable components and shuts everything down. Anything connected to the grid is at high risk of severe damage and failing."

Brad then quickly explained that it is widely believed that the United States had previously used an Electromagnetic Pulse to take out the enemies' communications during the first day of both the Gulf War and the Iraq War. In both of these wars, it was not a nuclear bomb that was used, but rather a large conventional bomb specifically designed for taking out electronics in a regional area, such as a battlefield. This belief has never been proven, and the United States has never admitted to using a bomb of this type. The main evidence that this actually occurred is that in both wars, the enemy was badly beaten very quickly, and the main reason is that they could not communicate on the battlefield. It was only after the initial war started that the US military would go into the battlefield after the electromagnetic pulse had ended.

When Brad finished his explanation, he looked back at his friends, who were silent and in shock. Then Brad shouted, "We need to shut as much of the grid as possible down before the nuclear blasts."

Fortunately, Brad had cellular service and knew the right people back home to call. But he needed to be fast because the hypersonic missiles would be in place to detonate within 20 minutes or so. Brad first called the Lead Manager, who worked directly under the administrator for the western grid in Denver. He woke him up from sleep, and the Lead Manager was not happy. Brad quickly explained the situation, but the Lead Manager was unable to make a quick decision without agreement from his circle of advisors and other federal government leadership. Brad had no time to waste, and this conversation was waste, so he hung up abruptly and dialed in three of his coworkers, each located at one of the three AC-DC-AC converter stations mentioned earlier. Each of these guys was also sleeping at the time, but this time, they knew of the real-time consequences. An abrupt shutdown of these stations would cause ripple effects of power throughout the western grid, which would shut down many power transmission paths and ultimately shut down power to cities and towns throughout the country. This action would be deadly to those dependent on power, but fortunately, emergency backup power would restore power to hospitals, etc. Then, after the HEMP blast was finished, they could re-connect switchgear and get the converter stations operating again, with a lot of luck. This objective was the agreed plan anyway, but shutting down such a sophisticated piece of equipment would not be easy, and all three guys took off for the converter stations to start the process. In the meantime, Brad called a good work friend in the main Dispatch for this federal agency. Brad contacted Tim, who was working the late shift of this 24/7 operation. Tim was the manager of five others working that night, and all were experienced linemen from the past and had taken jobs in Dispatch for one reason or another (some due to injuries experienced on the job). These were high-paying jobs with horrible hours and were high-stress on many occasions, and this was one of those times. Tim took the news from Brad with shock but knew exactly what to do because Brad and Tim had actually talked about this scenario before. Tim took immediate action after getting off the phone with Brad and loudly talked to his dispatch personnel. He said, "The US is under attack now with HEMP missiles; we have just a few minutes to try to save as much of the western grid as possible. Isolate eastern Wyoming, western South Dakota, and the panhandle of Nebraska, and shut the system down now by opening the switchgear! Contact the power plants and start disconnecting now! Disconnect every switch you can within this area, and if we have time start disconnecting outside this area to save equipment." Opening switchgear disconnects sections of the transmission line, and therefore significantly reduces damaging photons that can travel down conductors.

The Dispatch team was experienced and knew the sequence of shutting down transmission paths very well. But this was going to be chaotic due to the lack of time. Fortunately, most of them knew power plant personnel in Wyoming, and calls went to several power plants in Gillette, Wheatland, and other smaller power plants in western Wyoming, and also the Black Hills and the panhandle of Nebraska.

Things were happening fast, and if seen from outer space, it would have appeared that large sections of Wyoming, South Dakota, and Nebraska were going dark.

With time running out, Brad made one more phone call. He called his boss in Gillette. Brad's boss immediately knew what to do, and after his short conversation with Brad, he called his counterparts in Western South Dakota and the Pan Handle of Nebraska. Then he hurriedly called every lineman, technician, and admin person in his group and simply said, "Get to your emergency radios now." Then the phone went dead.

CHAPTER 2 - THE BLASTS

The nuclear missiles detonated within a couple of minutes of each other. One was over Washington DC, and the blast of light could actually be seen from many states in the west because of its detonation at 100 miles above DC, although the atmosphere dulled the light from this distance. The middle blast occurred above Rushville, Nebraska, probably because it was midway between the nuclear launch sites associated with F.E. Warren Air Force Base and the military installations in the Omaha metro area. The third blast detonated 100 miles above the midpoint between Edward's Air Force Base, California, and Vandenberg Air Force Base, California. If a person was anywhere near these areas, it would have seemed as though the sun immediately turned on, except the light was severely intense. Anyone looking up at the stars at this time would have experienced permanent damage to their sight.

The three nuclear blasts were not the only ones. One more was detonated above London, England. Russia knew that any blast closer to its own country could take out some of its electronics, so it limited the locations to these four only. Russian scientists knew that some of its satellites could be affected, but it took countermeasures as available, and collateral damage was expected.

Within a second of the blasts, the lower 48 States were inundated with ultra-fast photons, destroying transformer controls, and internet servers, and other equipment connected to long conductors or wiring.

Russia was successful in its planned attack. Now, what was their plan? Was Russia expecting support from Iran, North Korea, or China? Perhaps, but there was only silence for now, probably waiting for the next move by the United States. What Russia didn't know at the time was that the United States already had protocols for this type of event, and it was underway even before the blasts.

CHAPTER 3 - COUNTERMEASURES

The Russian government and military were trying to get the edge for what could have been World War Three. The Russian government wanted to cripple the United States so that its strength would be substantially less than what Russia had, and then, with support from Iran, North Korea, and hopefully China, the World Order would shift in their favor and allow for the rebuilding of the original land mass of the former USSR. It would also give China the green light to take control of Taiwan and, as a result, strengthen the Russian-China relationship. Also, secretly, some senior officials from Russia were in conversations with radical members of Germany who had aspirations of a Fourth Reich that would reassemble a greater Germany to what it was during the Roman Empire. But this wasn't meant to be. The United States was ready with its own hypersonic HEMP missiles, and they were thermonuclear. Six of these missiles were launched from various locations five minutes before the blast from the Russian HEMP missiles. The US government had great intelligence on this Russian operation and had suspected this attack for several months. The six missiles were strategic to cover all of Russia.

An elaborate and ultra-secret protocol was in place and was actively being started by the United States. Teams of high-level ambassadors were on landline phones with counterparts in Iran and China (the United States did not know about conversations with German officials at this time). The message was simple. The nuclear HEMP missiles will do nothing to hurt or even hinder the United States military. All military installations, naval vessels, and even some space satellites were hardened and undamaged. Any attempt to take advantage of the United States or its allies would be subject to an immediate reprisal of momentous means. "Stay away and stay out of this conflict."

The word "Hardened" is used in this case to describe the physical protection of military weapons and infrastructure from electromagnetic radiation. Hardened is derived from the use of a Faraday Cage, which is basically a protective structure that shields critical infrastructure from electromagnetic waves. You probably have a Faradays Cage in your house right now. It is a microwave oven, and it breaks up the microwave frequency into non-harmful radiation. However, the Faradays Cage needed to stop ultra-high frequency photons would need much smaller cage openings. It gets complicated for protection from super high-frequency photons, but the military and federal government have been working on solutions since the 1990s, and funding has been secretly flowing since then. In addition, all military installations had developed separate power microgrids. These microgrids were connected to the larger community power grids but also had quick break-away switchgear separating them from the main grids, and this was activated as soon as the Russian missiles were detected in Alaska. As a result, all military installations were off of the main grids during the blasts, and only emergency generators and backup battery power were available to critical operations during this time. Once the nuclear blasts occurred and the HEMP danger was over, the installations could reconnect to the main grid if the larger grids were undamaged. Unfortunately, in most instances, this was not the case, so military installations maintained emergency and battery backup power for indefinite periods. But at least they were fully functional and ready for battle if needed, and some were needed now.

Concurrent with the telephone calls by the ambassadors, thousands of stealthy and ultra-supersonic missiles were launched at specific military targets in Russia and North Korea. These missiles were so fast that Russia's defensive missile systems would not even come close to bringing them down. In preparation for this type of attack on Russia, the United States had identified and continually updated key targets that they wanted to take out, given the opportunity. That opportunity just happened, and the United States of America was to take full advantage of the moment. Civilian populations were not targets, but some collateral civilian deaths were unfortunately possible and even probable. It was not the Russian people who were the enemies; only the Russian government and military were.

The size and importance of the target determined the size of each US missile. High-value targets received multiple, large non-nuclear explosions, while targets such as vehicle storage areas received conventional explosions. But before the costly supersonic missiles were launched, conventional missiles were sent so that the US could see where Russia's defenses were. The United States had several locations that specifically watched the entire land mass of Russia so that Russian defenses could be spotted in real time. The data and information from these secret US locations were fed directly to two Headquarters command centers at Vandenberg Air Force Base, California, and NORAD in Colorado Springs, Colorado. These facilities were dual backup locations to one another, but the final decisions came from another location just east of Colorado Springs, Colorado, which is Space Force Headquarters. The Space Force is the same thing as the previously named Space Command within the Air Force.

Data and images poured in, and new targets were assigned in real-time. This action resulted in a second wave of ultra-supersonic and stealthy missiles toward Russia. This process repeated multiple times until the United States military and both political parties were satisfied at the subcommittee level within both the Senate and House of Representatives. This operation was considered a one-off situation, so satisfying both political parties was deemed necessary going forward. Surprisingly, both political parties had similar wish lists and agendas. Neither was softer than the other. Both political parties were sick of the many nuclear threats from the Russian Dictator and North Korea and wanted to end these dictatorships. Also, it was no secret that the people within these countries wanted the freedoms that the West had. The Russian people were not uninformed and knew of the abuses by the Russian Dictator and his Oligarchs. Too much money was skimmed off taxes from the Russian people and businesses. Corruption exists in all governments, including the United States, but corruption in Russia was nearly in the open, and the Russian people were sick and tired of it.

People worldwide took protective measures. No one knew what was going to happen except the upper leadership of the United States, including the military and defense subcommittees. However, corruption exists within the United States, too, so the FBI and CIA monitored the "Political Types" on both sides of the aisle. Fortunately, the political hacks on both sides of politics took a break from bashing the other side. Even the cable network SHTY tried to report fully accurate news that was evenly represented by both the Republicans and Democrats, but power was down for broadcasts. Unfortunately, some of the smaller pod-casts and shit-stations on both sides of the political spectrum tried to keep up political BS, but power was out in most of the country so the messages did not get out. The vast majority of the United States, however, were clearly behind the American defensive efforts.

The Internet worldwide was on fire with interest, with the exception of the areas of the world that were destroyed or crippled by high-speed electromagnetics. Communications in real-time were available unless the site was overrun, so this was the test of modern communications and how the world would react to knowing what was happening and why. Of course, the rumors ran wild, and conspiracy theories were developed and propagated, but it didn't take long for the truth to be learned. The United States was taking direct and absolute action. No more was this powerful country going to take the crap that it took for so many decades.

The counterattack by the United States was immediate. Within 24 hours, the entire Russian military complex was targeted, and the vast majority was being destroyed. A small number of government facilities were allowed to remain for any future new government, but an unconditional surrender was demanded from all current government personnel, starting at the top. These first 24 hours laid the groundwork for five full day & night attacks. Wave among a wave of US missiles came from every direction, including NATO. Nothing was spared. The United States and its allies knew that this was a once-in-a-lifetime situation and would not happen again, so every counterattack plan was initiated. It was hell-on-earth for Russia and North Korea. Those were the only countries targeted, and they were targeted heavily. China was not in the cross-hairs, but most people knew the threat from China was much different.

The Russian military, as well as North Korea, tried to retaliate, but nothing was left in their military arsenal that could reach any US targets. North Korea tried to hit South Korea, but every missile they launched was taken out over North Korea territory. The war in Ukraine had taken its toll on the Russian military, and the lack of good maintenance on installations and equipment had taken its toll as well. Also, the United States and its allies had anti-missile weapons placed at key locations in which they knew Russia would retaliate. Technology was much more advanced on the side of the United States and its allies. Russia thought of itself as equal to the United States in technology, and the United States encouraged this, but the truth is that Russia was more of a 3rd world country to the United States, with the exception of the nuclear weapons that Russia still had.

World War Three was adverted for now, and other countries stopped short of any aggressive action due to early warnings from the US ambassadors. Now, it was time to keep the peace worldwide and save Americans from the damage done by the Russian HEMP blasts.

CHAPTER 4 - THE DEVASTATION

Unfortunately, most of the US was in a bad way, without power and communications, and the supply chain was completely broken. Water, food, and fuel would soon be in short supply. Looting and lawlessness were inevitable. If you had a gun and ammo, you might be able to protect your house and property if attacked.

Over the first days, many neighborhoods developed security teams for protection, and this helped keep residential areas safer, but commercial areas were not as safe, particularly in cities with over 50,000 people. Protection for these areas became impossible, given that the HEPM blasts had taken out most of the communication. Governors even tried to activate the National Guard, but communication was nearly nonexistent. It was the Wild West and Wild East all over again. Both the western grid and eastern grid were severely damaged, and the Texas grid was also in shambles.

Local governments struggled everywhere, and it took a couple of days before some city and county workers showed up at work. Most government employees have reasonably stable incomes because the funding comes from taxes, so most employees knew they would get paid, and this helped keep towns and cities a little safer and cleaner. Most everyone knew the power would come back on soon, but nobody knew exactly what "soon" meant. Some people thought a day or so, but others were not that optimistic.

Whatever the case, cities needed to survive on what they had on hand, and fortunately, most towns and cities kept extra fuel, and this fuel was dedicated to the most critical needs.

All cities had skeleton crews working the utilities. The drinkable (potable) water systems lost pressure as soon as the supply tanks drained dry. This lost pressure means that the entire system needed to be considered contaminated. Any pressure line with less than five pounds per square inch was said to allow contamination from nearby soils or groundwater. Basically, this was the entire water system. But until power is restored, the city workers in this utility maintained and cleaned equipment so that the system could come back faster once activated again.

The sanitary sewer system is mostly gravity-drained, but lift stations are also commonplace. A lift station is exactly what it sounds like; it lifts sewage up such that it can again be gravity-drained. This action happens before the sewage gets to a treatment facility. But without power, the sewage just drains until it can't drain anymore. Lift stations normally have ponds built for about an hour or so if power goes out. This type of design allows city personnel to make necessary repairs before the pond fills with sewage. However, the ponds at lift stations are not designed for any more than an hour or so. Days or weeks without power would mean that sewage would overflow the pond and naturally seek lower elevations and this meant that sewage just kept draining to the lowest elevation, and this included neighborhoods.

Natural gas worked until pressures were reduced too much. This lack of pressure affected any household fixtures that required gas so it was fortunate that this event happened in late summer when heating requirements were not necessary.

Other areas of devastation or critical operation are....

AIRCRAFT: The electronics aboard aircraft were affected if they were not shielded in some way, particularly microelectronics. Within seconds of the blast, critical electronics were damaged, and with little time to correct the problems, many large airlines were brought to the ground due to a lack of control during the most critical time of these flights, take-off or landing. Aircraft in flight also had electronic damage, but pilots and crew members had more time to make adjustments. Commercial airliners are already built to correct failures with redundancy parts. Failures are typically in three main areas:

1. Emergency parts that wear out over time and have statistical lives. These types of failures are changed out regularly before the statistical failure occurs. Also, spare parts are carried on the aircraft in case a failure happens before the statistical average.

2. Emergency parts that fail without warning. These failures are corrected by having at least one other part already in place as a substitute for the failed part. A third and fourth substitute part may also exist on the aircraft.

3. Non-emergency parts that fail. These parts can be changed after landing the aircraft.

The HEMP blast did take out emergency electronics, but backup parts kicked in after the HEMP blast had passed. In addition, the outer shell of the airliners was a sort of Faraday's Cage and stopped much of the damaging photons. Cable wiring within some airliners were also shielded by design so as not to allow damaging photons to attach to the wiring. Older aircraft had an advantage over newer models in that mechanical and hydraulic cabling was often used for flight control. The newer aircraft had more electronics, but wire shielding did occur on many.

It was horrific to see airplane crashes in many major cities. Fortunately, in many older aircraft with cabling for flight controls, as long as the fuel pumps operated, they could be brought down safely. Every airplane in the United States came down one way or the other, but the vast majority of them landed safely.

Communications with towers were immediately out, so every aircraft was on its own for landing if it could. In some situations, the landing runways were crash sights, so in these cases, other airplanes went to other airports or took to freeways or other open fields. If an airplane did make it safely to the ground, no services were available, so emergency slides were deployed. Fortunately, aircraft can survive lightning strikes, so the design that went into this area was a godsend for many large aircraft. Also, the Hardening of aircraft was already being implemented into the design, so many newer models with more microelectronics survived the blast.

Smaller aircraft were less affected because cabling for wing controls was generally used rather than electronic components. If landing gear was fixed or already down, this made for better odds of safe landing.

There seemed to be no single answer on how an aircraft would be affected because some of the same types of aircraft would be less affected than others of the exact same type and year. It must have been the position of the aircraft during the blast that affected some while not affecting others, or perhaps the matter in the atmosphere made some difference, reducing the damaging photons. However, hundreds of aircraft were affected during the blast, and the experienced crew saved the vast majority of airplanes. It was fortunate that the blasts happened at nighttime when fewer aircraft were in the sky.

INTERNET, COMPUTERS, and ELECTRONIC DEVICES: Servers, computers, and other electronic devices were more likely to fail if connected to power or other electronic cabling, but if the device was turned off during the blast, no damage would occur. It was for this reason that these nighttime blasts had a lower effect on many cell phones or other mobile devices. However, main-frame computers and internet servers were generally affected nationwide. It seemed to be hit-or-miss, but it was actually where the device was located, and how it was positioned. In any case, communication via the Internet was offline for weeks.

BANKING AND CRIPTO CURRENCY: With electric power down in most of the country, bank computers could not communicate with ATMs (Automated Teller Machines). Cash money was in most ATMs, but people couldn't access them for money unless they could connect to servers confirming identity and bank information. Cash was becoming the main way to purchase anything within the United States, so this amplified the problem.

Cryptocurrency was another issue. Worldwide, Cryptocurrency was alive and well, with the exception of Russia and the lower 48 states of America and this meant that if anyone could access the Internet, purchases could still be made, and trading could still happen because the seller would be assured of getting the money when the power was finally restored.

Many people wanted to make trades or purchases with credit cards, and some did take paper receipts this way, but a lot of sellers would shy away from this type of transaction.

Basically, cash was king for purchase and trading during the weeks that power was out.

HEALTHCARE FACILITIES: Hospitals, Emergency Care Facilities, Senior Residences, and other critical facilities did have emergency generators for as long as they had fuel, but after a week or so, most of these ran out of fuel and this meant that patients who needed electronic equipment either struggled for life or died. It was absolutely horrific in all hospitals throughout the lower 48 states of America. Death was overtaking America in facilities like these. But it wasn't just current patients that had critical needs.

Everyone uses hospitals and emergency care services. Accidents happen all the time, and they escalated during this event. Healthcare was needed everywhere. Fortunately, it was in this occupation that many people were extremely dedicated. Nurses, doctors, and other emergency care staff showed up at their place of employment to help as needed, and much was needed. But here again, there were limitations to materials, supplies, and medicine. Anesthesia was in short supply, and when it started to run out, it was like the 1800s for pain when operations were necessary. Doctors were considering anything that could help, even alcohol.

If a person died at home, and the city could not be contacted, the family needed to take things into their own hands and bury their loved one in the backyard. We have grown accustomed to the specialization of jobs and tasking. So, when life goes back to the ways of the 1800's, it is a shocking realization.

FIRES: It wasn't just looting that devastated communities because fires went uncontrolled. Water flowed as long as elevated tanks had water, but this only lasted for a day or so because pumps and motors were inactive without the needed electric power. It seemed as though every city in the United States was on fire somewhere. Many high-rise buildings have their own supply of water for fires. Large tanks are placed on or near the roof areas. Every building is different, and a lot of factors go into how fire control is designed and constructed. Supertall high-rise buildings have many zones, but everything is controlled by electronics so this became the number one threat to those living in tall buildings and even mid-rise buildings. A knowledgeable Home Owners Association (HOA) and on-site Stationary Engineer could get a handle on this, but in the vast majority of cases, this was not to be.

With no electricity or gas for fireplaces or barbeques, some started to cook using wood or paper products. Most of the time, this worked with smoke spilling out of patio doorways. Unfortunately, there are those in the city who don't know how to operate open flames in a safe way. In some cases, fires got out of control and spread quickly to other floors. In most of these cases, neighbors tried to help, knowing the consequences if they didn't help. High-rise fires were in most large cities, and the Fire Department was not able to help. It was simply heartbreaking to watch people struggle to gain control and then realize that they were doomed. As you can imagine, many people jumped to their deaths during high-rise fires. Gunshots could also be heard, and it was assumed that suicide was committed, but most people struggled to the end, and most were overcome by smoke inhalation, which was much better than burning alive.

Downtown areas without tall buildings were also at risk because many buildings were so close together. If fires occurred here, fire brigades were established if enough people volunteered.

Fires were everywhere in neighborhoods, and some block-homes were totaled. Neighbors worked to control fires as best as can be expected, and here again, fire brigades were created. This action worked in some cases, but other areas just burned from one residence to another. Many cities and towns were on fire for weeks.

COMMUNICATIONS: Communication was a big problem on all levels of government, but no more than with cities and towns, where hands-on and boots-on-the-ground mean life or death. Walkie-talkies, CB (citizen band) radios, and Ham radios became some methods of communication since cell coverage was mostly out. The CB radio is more for personal communication, and the Ham radios are for long distances. But distance was still an obstacle for other than small towns or utilities that had their own established channels.

It generally took a full day and night for volunteers and city workers to show up to help out. Most people with families could not help because they had their own personal family issues. But in most communities, some turned up to help out. It's amazing how Americans step up when needed, and this was certainly one of those times.

Communication was one of the many "number one priorities" of federal and state governments. Temporary generators were dispatched to cell towers and radio towers based on usage, and all of them would eventually get attention. This requirement would take weeks to complete, but this was an ongoing operation and fuel for communication-type vehicles was authorized by all levels of government, right up there with food, water, and medicine distribution.

SANITARY AND STREET CITY WORKERS: In large cities with dense populations, the city employees who showed up for sanitary cleanup and road maintenance had the gruesome task of collecting dead bodies and transporting them to mass burial sites. With no power, they had no refrigeration, so something needed to be done with the dead. All cities and towns had some level of this situation, and the general solution was to gather the best information about the dead and then bury them in known locations so that they could be relocated after things got back to normal. Large parks and other open areas were used in this way. It was the best and most respectful thing that could be done, other than cremation, and cremation was not an option due to fuel, but these facilities also depended on electricity.

TRANSPORTATION AND FUEL: Most local governments had their own supply of fuel for vehicles. However, it was not known when these supplies would be replenished. The federal government had huge surplus oil supplies, but refined fuel was needed now, so the federal government made oil refineries another priority.

It was the good neighboring countries that really saved the United States when it came to fuel. Both Mexico and Canida began immediate truck and flight deliveries as long as there were security escorts. For this reason, the federal government of the United States has placed fuel for security as another one of the growing "number one priorities." Unlike other "number one priorities," this one was critical for food, water, communications, medicine, etc. In a way, it was the number one priority of the "number one priorities."

FOOD, WATER, AND MEDICINE: Food and water were other critical priorities. Water was more of a priority, but depending on where you lived in the United States, that could be argued. Most communities had some access to both food and water, but this largely depended on where you lived and the population. It was very difficult, but after the first two weeks, some communication was achieved; priorities were communicated via satellite phones or emergency radio networks for airdrops from Mexico and Canada.

DEATH, SUFFERING, and RELOCATING: Death was everywhere, and life for the living was getting worse. Clean supplies were diminishing, and food was running out fast. As this happened, large populations traveled to more rural areas, the mountains, and the coasts to survive. This mass migration of people caused gun fights as everyone became more desperate.

The president of the United States and Congress quickly learned that only one major area of the United States was basically unharmed and fully functional with power. That is why it was a no-brainer to consider relocating the federal government to Ellsworth Air Force Base and Rapid City. After this occurred, word slowly got out that the Black Hills had power. This news caused many to try to reach this area. However, they could only go as far as the gas in their vehicle would take them. Even if they made it to the Black Hills, they would have found problems. The supply chain was gone, and local residents were hunkering down with whatever supplies they had, but given this was rapidly becoming the new location for the federal government, supplies were being received through a constant stream of aircraft at Ellsworth Air Force Base, as well as the Rapid City Airport. The military was establishing strong control and created an outer parameter around the populated areas of Rapid City and out to Ellsworth Air Force Base. Congress, with their families, were being transported to this area, and motels were becoming their temporary residences. The population of Rapid City doubled within a week, but this did not include tent communities that were developed around the city by people who made it to this area but were not allowed in. The government provided these communities food and water so they didn't infiltrate Rapid City and Ellsworth Air Force Base. This effort created a safer environment for the many incoming families from Congress and the federal government.

GOOD NEIGHBORS: Both Canada and Mexico experienced some destruction from the blasts, but both nations recuperated fast and organized missions to help the United States. It was an amazing switch of roles, in which the United States used to be the one sending help, not the other way around. North and South America united with help, and help was coming fast from other NATO countries as well. Coastal airstrips were quickly adapted to receive aircraft, re-fuel them, and then safely have them take off for another round of supplies. Saying that this was similar to the Berlin Air Lift was an understatement because it was happening in cities on the Pacific

Coast, Atlantic Coast, Gulf Coast, northern border with Canada, southern border with Mexico, and many large cities within the United States. It was an effort that shocked the world. Unfortunately, large transformers would take years to re-supply, but smaller ones came in by the airplane and container ships.

South Korea, the main supplier of large transformers, immediately started manufacturing large transformers even without purchase orders. They knew they would be needed. Even workers in these facilities came in to work, without guarantee of pay. They knew that it was the right thing to do.

The United States made it clear that supplies would be reimbursed and tabulations would be kept, but no free country in the world would stop needed shipments to the United States during their time of need.

China also contributed. You see, China and the United States have a very unique relationship, and both countries know that the relationship can't fail. Both countries have too much to lose, so China was a major contributor when it came to aid to the United States.

CHAPTER 5 - BACKGROUND OF LEARNING

The Power Grid can be thought of as the largest man-made living being on earth, with tens of thousands of humans maintaining it and keeping it alive. It takes this many people to keep the power supply equalized with demand and at the frequency of 60 hertz. When the power grid was re-energized in the smaller and isolated areas of eastern Wyoming, western South Dakota, and the panhandle of Nebraska, it naturally did not have the same supply needs. For this reason, this area slowly gained some power, and then it dropped, and this went on for several days until the power plants and supply were normalized. It was touch and go for a long time, but the dispatch, power personnel, and field crews were the best on earth, and power slowly was reestablished.

To make matters worse, nobody had good communication with anyone else due to the HEMP blasts, but they did have walky-talkies and CB radios, which helped some. It was experience that helped everyone involved to understand the process. Almost everyone had taken a Power Grid class in Golden, Colorado, and it was this class that helped everyone understand the enormous task of getting power going again.

The federal agency's headquarters that Brad worked for was in Denver, Colorado. Management for this federal agency had started in the Denver Federal Center in Lakewood, Colorado, where the federal government already owns the land and utilities, but the senior leadership soon wanted their own separate space. They leased the 41st floor in an expensive high-rise in downtown Denver and then tried to rent cheap space for the dispatch location that was currently in Lakewood, Colorado. This attempt to move dispatch by senior leadership was quickly abandoned when most of the good Engineers, Technicians, and IBEW personnel objected. For this reason, management agreed to move dispatch to Gillette. Also, the rent was much cheaper in Gillette, so the high cost of leasing a full floor of a high-rise would be less noticeable to Congress, the Department of Energy, and the general public.

The decisions made during this HEMP attack were not made easily. But Brad and the others involved were as prepared as best as possible. This preparation started a few years earlier.

Three years before this HEMP attack, Brad had become concerned about an attack of this sort. He brought it up to the senior leadership of his federal power administration, but all they did was say that the Department of Energy would take care of this if needed. Basically, they brushed his concerns off. A few months later, he tried again but was told to stay in his own space and that it was not his concern. Brad wasn't the kind to be ignored like this; in fact, it made him stronger in his intent, and he went back to his field office in Gillette and arranged the first Friday afternoon meeting with all the linemen and technicians in his group.

Brad wasn't the only one who experienced problems with senior leadership of this particular federal sub-agency (under the Department of Energy). The International Brotherhood of Electrical Workers (IBEW), which represents the lineman for this federal agency, had issues with leadership not following through with many promises from the past. It became evident that some rogue senior leadership for this federal agency looked at the field crews as simple labor and this caused extremely bad feelings. It was for this reason that negotiators were sent from IBEW headquarters. These negotiators were given full authority and had solid relationships with senior personnel at the Department of Energy. Members from IBEW are in all areas of the federal government, and with the exception of this federal power administration, good relations existed. When the negotiators from IBEW HQ learned of the underhanded tactics used against their members, they decided to pull out the stops. They put together the best team of negotiators and researched all issues in full. The very next negotiations occurred in Gillette, and senior leadership for this power company didn't know what hit them. First, the lead negotiator for IBEW started with a joke. The particulars of this joke aren't important, but what was important was that the joke's conclusion basically called federal leadership a bunch of cowards. This joke shocked everyone on both sides of the meeting, but what was more shocking was how the senior leadership took it. They had odd smiles on their faces and said nothing, not even defending themselves. That's when the IBEW negotiators knew they had the upper hand. They brought up each and every issue in detail and demanded a full response in writing. Senior management tried to resist, and that's when the IBEW negotiators explained that the good relations with the Department of Energy (DOE) could be severely damaged. As it happened, the management of this federal sub-agency worked for the Department of Energy, and their tone changed immediately. Management apologized and said that they could address each problem, and IBEW was assured that any issues would be corrected immediately. Nothing more was needed, but IBEW wanted to flex its muscles a little and demanded that management provide Gatorade for all field personnel every workday. This demand was an over-the-top demand, but management buckled immediately. Then, the meeting ended. That was three years ago, and things improved a little, but the HEMP issues remained unaddressed.

The Friday meeting that Brad set up was very informal and was the last couple hours of the week for most of the workers in his group. Brad raised his concern and was pleasantly surprised that others were also concerned. Safety and grounding were always discussed throughout the year, but nothing was ever said about electromagnetic pulse issues, and this kicked off a good discussion. Every week, more was brought up and learned of the HEMP issues, and this fueled many to research it further. Reports were found on the Internet from several departments in the federal government, and many were just being released from a contractor for the United States from Santa Barbara County, California, so this was very current information for both safety and security.

From a security perspective, the group discussed many scenarios in which the grid could be taken down, not just by a HEMP. Much of the discussion revolved around the security of substations and the long transmission lines in rural lands and this launched an active and energetic conversation on how the grid can be damaged and, as a result, how to protect it. The conversation was almost a challenge on who could come up with the best or easiest way to take the western grid down so that they could find solutions on how to protect it and their wellbeing, too. Brad had thought about this a lot over the years, so he put his plan out there. Brad had read of other blackouts and brownouts over the years and learned that most were due to vegetation overgrowth or simple mistakes. One was in 2010 in the southwest, and it was caused by a simple mistake that even took out a nuclear power plant in California (this nuclear power plant was decommissioned after this event). The report of this outage detailed every microsecond of the events leading to the outage, and it was this report that gave Brad much of his ideas. Here they are.....

Brad explained that several key substations needed to be damaged within a few hours to take out the western grid. First, the western grid must be separated from any backup power from the eastern grid and this meant that a couple of the AC-DC-AC converter stations identified earlier needed to be taken offline. This action could be done in several ways. These stations were highly sophisticated and complicated. Parts were difficult to come by because most of the high technology came from Germany. Brad explained how the Sydney station could be taken down easily. Brad explained that after this was accomplished, the Stegall station could be damaged by putting a couple of bullets in the bottom of the largest transformer oil tank. The oil would slowly drain out, and the transformer would be critically damaged if not noticed in time. The sound of a gunshot would not alarm anyone in these parts.

While the oil slowly drained from the Stegall transformer, the terrorists would drive to Rapid City or Denver for a quick trip to Phoenix. Once in Phoenix, the terrorist would have a pre-parked truck nearby, in the airport parking lot, or a short Uber ride away. The truck would include a catapult capable of launching two metallic hooks attached by a semi-flexible conductor, similar to the conductors on a 230kV transmission line. The terrorist would have tested this catapult many times for distance and height to fling it across the three phases of an AC transmission line or the two conductors of a DC transmission line. If ground or neutral wires were in place above the power conductors, the entire hook & cable device would be flung over them all. The middle conductor (or phase) would not be touched, but at least two phases would be out.

The terrorist would have pre-planned locations that were very remote to launch the catapult. The terrorist would have planned the locations based on the detailed map of the western power grid that was readily available through Western Electric Coordinating Council (WECC). Locations would be chosen for maximum outages, and many remote locations exist in Arizona and California.

Once the terrorist was successful in the first catapult launch, he (or she) would travel up to the Tracy

Substation in California. This location is rural but has a small scattered population nearby, so any catapult launch here would definitely be late at night. Immediately after this catapult launch, the terrorist would make one final catapult launch onto what is referred to as Path 25. This large transmission line was installed after the Enron outage in the 2000s.

Basically, power on the western grid can be thought of as flowing clockwise, from the Northwest (Oregon, Washington) to Idaho, Montana, Wyoming, North Dakota, South Dakota, Nebraska, Kansas, Oklahoma, Colorado, Utah, New Mexico, Nevada, and Arizona, and then into the black hole of power consumption, Southern California. The remaining left-over power would finally see it to the Bay Area and Sacramento, but with occasional blackouts. It is for this reason that Path 25 was developed. It is a direct transmission feed from the Northwest hydropower to Northern California. With this brief explanation, Brad said that the terrorist would make one more catapult launch in a rural area of Path 25 and that once this is accomplished, the western grid would be mostly down. Dispatch would try to back-feed the looped power grid to large population areas, but with so many outages, little could be done to get the western grid back online.

After Brad's description, everyone attending that Friday's meeting was astonished. One guy loudly stated, "Holy Shit, that's really possible". Brad then explained that solutions needed to be developed to counter this kind of terrorist. Brad said they would not get any help from the administrator's Lead Manager or his cronies and needed to implement any counter-terrorist plans themselves. Immediately, suggestions for cameras, extra patrols, signage, etc., were made, but it was late evening, so they tabled the suggestion for the following Friday.

The following Friday was a packed house. Engineers came in from Rapid City, South Dakota, Cheyenne, Wyoming, and Casper, Wyoming, and even other power companies had linemen and technicians in attendance. Two power companies that had attendees were Black Hills Public Power and SoDak Power. Both of these companies are known as excellent employers who treat their employees with respect and value and this creates a sense of teamwork that produces better and safer design and maintenance practices.

NOTE: The terms SoDak and NoDak were created in the 1960s, short for South Dakota and North Dakota.

These Friday meetings were becoming a big deal, and many good contacts were made. It was these contacts that helped Brad when the need occurred during the HEMP attack, and it was these meetings that helped those in attendance to fully understand the critical needs of that day.

CHAPTER 6 - BRAD AND THE TEAM TRAVEL

Brad and his friends witnessed the long-distance blast that occurred over California, but fortunately, the atmosphere between Alaska and California was enough to keep Alaska unharmed. It seems being close to Russia was an advantage in this case.

Now it was time to get back home, and fortunately, the grid was becoming operational in this area, thanks to Brad's quick phone calls and the actions from Dispatch, as well as the guys at the three AC-DC-AC converter stations. As Brad and his friends returned the rental boat, they began to get some news from the lower 48 states. It was good to hear that most of the Black Hills, eastern Wyoming, and the panhandle of Nebraska were in good shape, with power coming from Gillette, Wheatland, and Rapid City.

It was clear from the limited news that the power was off in many of the areas that Brad and his friends needed to travel through to get to Gillette and Rapid City. Even southern Canada was affected a little. For this reason, Brad decided to rent a four-wheel drive double cab pickup and travel towards Saskatoon, Saskatchewan, Canada. Then, Brad and his friends would stock up on gas with many extra gallons stored in the truck bed and head south through Moose Jaw, Canada, to Gillette. After that, Brad would be home, and his friends would continue with the vehicle to Rapid City. It was a simple plan, but the trip had many unknowns. They didn't know how accessible gas would be during the trip, and nobody knew what conditions they would encounter on the way. In any case, they loaded the truck with their supplies and left Anchorage by morning.

The trip started well because this area was completely unaffected by the blast, but the news coming from southern Canada and the lower 48 states was shocking. This news gave them a warning that they should stock up on supplies and cash before driving south to Wyoming. Some ATMs were working, so they all maxed out on cash removals. Fortunately, they all had camping gear and sleeping bags, but they did stock up on food and clean water. They also had three large coolers stuffed with salmon and other fish fillets that were packed in ice. The truck rental was the right decision because they loaded up the back of the truck as they traveled. They would drive 24 hours per day, switching off drivers while others slept.

The Drive to Whitehorse, Canada, was so beautiful that they all were able to get the horrors of the recent past out of their minds. Brad even mentioned that next year, they should drive up to a Canadian lake for a full week of camping and fishing, and this helped with a fun and active conversation until they saw a long line of campers and other vehicles traveling in the opposite direction. It looked like a traffic jam of slow-moving recreational vehicles going to Alaska or other northwest parts of Canada. This traffic made sense once they saw it happening, but nobody anticipated it. It was this unexpected event that caused Brad to suggest that they try to anticipate upcoming events. What were they to expect as they got closer to home? The string of recreational vehicles stretched as far as they could see, and at night, it was a sight to behold. Fortunately, Brad was not experiencing any traffic in the direction they were going, so he kept his speed somewhat high. However, he was also aware of large animals crossing the highway or an impatient driver passing slower vehicles in the opposite direction. Occasionally, they'd see a vehicle breakdown, but that was rare. Between Prince George and Edmonton, Canada, Brad noticed a well-built home that was off the highway about a mile. It had many tall antenna towers on the roof, and that meant a long-range CB and Ham radio operator lived there. Brad noticed it because he was looking for a safe place to rest for a few hours and also wanted some possible communication with those back home. Every one of them was bushed, and trading off driving wasn't helping that much. It must have been the stress of the last day or so, plus the worry of loved ones back home.

Brad pulled up in the gravel driveway and was greeted by three barking dogs, showing teeth. The barking alerted the homeowner, who came out the door holding a double-barrel shotgun. He also had an obvious side-arm pistol. The homeowner had his dogs back up and yelled at Brad and the others, "What you want?". Brad had his window down and explained that they were traveling from Alaska to Wyoming and the Black Hills. Brad then explained that they were just looking for a safe place to sleep for a few hours.

The homeowner was Troy, and he heard everything Brad said. He just stared at them for a full minute, suspicious. That's when Brad made an offer. Brad said he'd trade his cooler of fish with Troy if they could just park there for a while.

Troy was intrigued and could see what Brad said made sense, so he asked to see the cooler. Troy healed the dogs, and Brad got out of the truck and showed Troy the cooler. The sight of those fish fillets was all it took for Troy to change his demeanor, and he then welcomed Brad and the guys. Troy showed them where to park, which had a nice grassy area for setting up a tent or just sleeping under the stars. All of the guys pulled out sleeping bags, and it wasn't long before snoring was heard. Before Brad joined them, he had one more important thing to do. He asked about the antennas.

For the next couple of hours, Brad and Troy sat around an elaborate setup of electronic boxes with wiring all about the room. All of this equipment was connected to heavy duty surge protectors to safeguard against strong solar flares, so this shielded against the HEMP blast as well. Troy told Brad of the news he was hearing from southern Canada and the United States. They were drinking beers, too, making the conversation pleasant and comfortable. Troy explained that he was part of a network of CB and Ham Radio operators in both Canada and the United States. Troy told some horror stories of frantic people in many areas, but he went into detail about one report in Denver, Colorado. Troy heard of large gang-like groups that were terrorizing much of the inner city. Violent crimes like rape, murder, and even torture were being reported. One of his CB and Ham Radio friends in an area near Federal Boulevard and

West Colfax Avenue in Denver recorded some sounds of the previous day. It sounded like a war with screams and automatic weapons. Troy even contacted this individual while Brad was there and got an update on the events. While they were talking to Troy's friend, gunshots were heard, and then nothing for a few seconds. Then, while Troy and Brad were listening, they heard several voices talking about grabbing all the food and any guns. What Troy and Brad were hearing was of gang members that violently barged into the house, shot and killed Troy's friend, and were in the process of stealing anything of value. Troy and Brad were shocked and helpless to assist, so they just listened to the house being ransacked until the gang left.

Troy then wrote his phone number and radio handle names on a piece of paper and handed them to Brad. Troy said, "You seem like a decent guy. When you get home, keep in touch with me on what's happening so I can update my radio network". Brad agreed and then went out to get some sleep for himself, although it was difficult to sleep hearing what he had just heard in Denver.

Early the next morning, Brad and the guys were off. They said their goodbyes to Troy and his good dogs, and Brad crashed in the back seat while the other guys started the trip back home.

It didn't take long before they entered the city of Edmonton, Canada, and Brad woke up with all of the excitement. The guys were shocked to see so much activity. Some people were actively boarding up windows, and many others were openly walking with guns. No gunshots were heard, though, and it seemed reasonably safe. Desperation didn't get this far north yet, and maybe it wouldn't, but the people of Edmonton were not taking any chances.

As they left Edmonton, Brad explained to the guys what was happening in Denver and what Troy had told him. Everyone was silent for about an hour after that, pondering what would come next.

Saskatoon, Canada, was just a few hours down the road, and then they would turn right, going south towards Moose Jaw, Canada, and the United States.

In Saskatoon, the situation was much like that in Edmonton. It was orderly, but you could see the concern in the faces of the people. They stopped at one large shopping center, which had ammo available. While two guys guarded the truck, the others went in to buy extra ammo, food, and bottled water. They came out with full shopping carts, and getting everything loaded on the truck was difficult. Then, they were on their way south to Moose Jaw.

It was uneventful going south, but streams of cars were still heading north and this wasn't a surprise anymore. The Canadian highway patrol was visible on this stretch of highway, and it appeared they were there to keep the flow of traffic moving.

When they reached the border between Canada and the United States, it became apparent why the highway patrol wanted the highway to run smoothly. The traffic going into the United States was easy for them, but the traffic stretched for miles northbound.

The Canadian National Police were doing everything possible to keep things moving, but it was chaotic on the United States side. On the American side, the highway patrol kept the peace, but people were frantic. Gas was obviously running low, and a gas tanker was in place to help out on the Canadian side.

It didn't take much to get into the United States. The highway patrol had its hands full with the northbound traffic. Brad and the guys showed their driver's licenses, and then they were waved in. That was the only easy thing on this trip so far. Now get through Montana and on to Gillette.

About an hour into Montana, Brad and the guys witnessed some serious desperation. One car was broken down and the two people from this vehicle were trying everything to get a ride north to Canada. Most vehicles slowed down some, but it was clear that everyone was afraid, and most vehicles would just speed off and this, in turn, caused a slowdown on the highway, and the two people from the abandoned vehicle would walk up close to each vehicle as they slowly moved forward.

At one point, the male from the abandoned vehicle started slamming his fist down on the hood of a blue sedan.

The driver of the blue sedan pulled out his pistol and shot one round into the sky, and this forced the person back a little, but he just went to his abandoned vehicle, pulled his own rife out, and started to walk back to the blue sedan while his wife frantically tried to stop him. That's when things went bad fast. The passenger of the blue sedan pulled out her pistol, and shots were fired from both sides.

The end results were two dead bodies lying on the highway.

This deadly event happened while Brad and the guys were driving cautiously past. It was surreal. After the killing, Brad stopped the truck, and three of the guys got out and carried the bodies to the broken-down vehicle. They could do little more given their serious situation, so they started back on the highway heading south to Wyoming. Brad tried to call the highway patrol to tell them about the dead bodies in the abandoned vehicle, but cell coverage was out.

It was a somber drive as they continued south, and the realism of this HEMP attack was sinking in fast. They talked about this shooting some, and most thought the people in the blue sedan had no choice. But the lady should not have been killed because she was not at fault. In other words, they witnessed a self-defense shooting as well as a murder. No pictures were taken during this shooting, so it would most likely go unsolved as just one more tragedy due to the Russian HEMP blasts. They were all quiet after this short conversation.

It didn't take long before they reached the Fort Peck Indian Reservation. At this border, the Rez Police had it blocked off in an attempt to protect the residents on the Rez (short for reservation). Brad stopped the truck and was met by three armed Rez police officers. They asked where Brad was going, and he explained the fishing trip in Alaska and the events that followed, including their destinations of Gillette and Rapid City. The Rez police became more comfortable with this explanation and explained some trouble on the highway just south of the Rez. They told of some gun fights, and that's when Brad said he had a trade for them to allow them to travel through the Rez. Brad offered one cooler full of salmon fillets and two large, full gas containers. This kind of surprised the Rez police, but they naturally accepted nonetheless. One Rez vehicle accompanied them, with Brad following in his truck, sped south, and easily made it through the Rez. When they reached the other side, they made the trade, and Brad gave the Rez police some of the food and water bottles, too. It was appreciated, and the Rez Police told them that they had heard of many more problems south in both Montana and Wyoming. The police heard that some vehicles were jacked up and shootings occurred but didn't know more than that; then Brad and the guys were off.

Brad and the guys made it to Interstate 94 and started towards Miles City when they saw the smoke ahead on the interstate. They approached with extreme caution and with loaded weapons. There appeared to be at least five vehicles burning with doors open, and that's when they saw the first two bodies. The Rez police were right about the gunfight, but it was over now. Nobody was alive, just burning cars that had been ransacked. What happened here wasn't known except that one group of people must have known what was being transported. Whatever happened here was over, and Brad and the guys maneuvered around the burning cars and continued on I-95 to Miles City, Montana, and then south to the Wyoming border and Gillette.

It was good to finally make it back to Gillette, and Brad was welcomed by his girlfriend, Ella. She hadn't had any contact with Brad for the past two days, but she knew he was a survivor, and she learned that he was headed home. When she saw the truck, she came out running, and several neighbors did, too. Brad was well respected in his neighborhood, and they all formed a tight-knit community. Brad and the guys unpacked everything except what was going to Rapid City, and they all felt safe for the first time in days. Gillette was safer than the vast majority of the United States and more prepared than most places. You see, Gillette might be in a solid four-season climate, but it is literally sitting on the cleanest coal reserves in the world. Just a few feet below the city is a 70-foot-thick coal formation, and it is sulfur-free, so it's very clean coal. The total extent of this massive reserve is still not known, but it was clearly a large swampy bog in historic times, and now it supplies several clean power plants in the area. Also, oil is found in this area. The Gillette area and Wyoming, in general, can be thought of as being energy-rich. Even yellowcake, a nuclear material, can be found about 100 miles south of Gillette. However, it is not just oil, clean (sulfur-free) coal, and nuclear material that make Wyoming rich in energy. Large wind-generating plants exist throughout Wyoming because of dependable winds for more than half the year. Solar fields are also planned for much of the southern parts of the state. In fact, several attempts have been made to have power generated in Wyoming to be sent directly to the southern part of California. One large project is under construction now.

It was late evening, so Brad's friends decided to get some real sleep and travel back to Rapid City early the next day. They spent the remainder of the evening talking about the happenings of the past few days and making plans for the future.

One of Brad's neighbors was a soft-spoken man nicknamed TJ, and he stayed quiet while the group settled. When the excitement settled a little, TJ looked at Brad and the others and said that he has been in contact with Troy up in Canada, as well as a couple of other CB and Ham Radio operators in the Black Hills, one in Sturgis and the other from Rapid City. He said that Troy got ahold of him just after Brad and company left and wanted to let his wife know they were on their way. Brad was a little shocked by this but let TJ continue. TJ said that something big was happening in Rapid City and the nearby Air Force Base. TJ didn't have the details but heard the federal government was setting up camp there and that getting into the city would be very difficult. TJ warned that every exit off Interstate 90 going into Rapid City would be blocked, but his CB and Ham radio friend in Rapid would contact the guards at the Deadwood Avenue exit to let them know that a few Rapid City residents were coming in from Gillette. This news was fantastic for Brad's fishing pals, and the next morning, they successfully made it home to Rapid.

After Brad spent a comfortable night with Ella and after his friends left for Rapid, he went to his office to see what was needed. Fortunately, his boss and the other linemen and technicians already had a handle on things, as best as can be expected anyway.

Maps covered all table tops, and red ink showed where work had been done in opening switchgear to isolate the working portions of the grid from the damaged areas. His coworkers and his boss were out the last couple of days making this happen and working with dispatch and the power operators to normalize power requirements. It was a heavy task, but these guys were the best, and the work they did after Brad's initial phone call while in Alaska made it a reality. It was a miracle that his office in Wyoming worked in coordination with their counterparts in Nebraska and South Dakota to isolate this large area, keeping power flowing.

After Brad's initial phone call to dispatch in Gillette, the dispatch manager (Tim) called Brad's boss. This action immediately set up a string of events with conversations between offices in Gillette, Rapid City, and Chadron, Nebraska, as well as other field offices in these regions. They only had a few minutes to talk, but it was made clear that the goal was to isolate the area of western South Dakota, the panhandle of Nebraska, and eastern Wyoming. With that goal in mind, the various offices pulled out large paper maps of their systems to determine which switchgear needed to be opened to isolate the planned areas.

Before the blast, the dispatch personnel were successful in opening switches that they had control over, but other switchgear was manual and needed a lineman to physically go to that site to open the mechanism. When the blast occurred, all of the manual switchgear was still closed, allowing power to flow, so it was not known what damage had occurred. It was wait and see if the power could come back after this area of Nebraska, South Dakota, and Wyoming was fully isolated.

Fortunately, the lineman still had communications with others in the area because they still had radios. A couple of years earlier, the administrator's Lead Manager wanted to save money by having all field personnel use cell phones and to get rid of the radios. But the IBEW stood up for the field personnel, stating the obvious: that cell coverage was not dependable in many remote areas and that some areas don't even have cell coverage. The Lead Manager should have known this, and it was obvious that he was out of touch with the real situation on the ground. In his office in Denver, cell phones are very dependable, but not so up in Wyoming or many areas in the Black Hills. The IBEW was successful in keeping these life-saving radios, and it helped greatly in completing power isolation.

Within a few hours, all switchgear was opened. Then, dispatch and the power plants started to power up this isolated part of the grid. All of the generation plants were in spinning reserve (reserve power generation that is available if needed), so they could put them online quickly, but in this delicate situation, they ramped up power slowly. By this time, field personnel were told to stay where they were and to observe any issues when power was being brought back online. If seen from space, it would have looked like a spiderweb of lights coming on in all three of these states. The lights would get dull and then become brighter again, and this would happen many times as the dispatch crew frantically worked to restore the system with help from experienced field personnel.

Most of this isolated system did come back, but there were problem areas where the manual switchgear wasn't opened in time. A few transformers were out of commission, and this affected three small communities. Fortunately, dispatch, with the help of field personnel, could back feed two of these areas. The third, in Lusk, Wyoming, required a temporary mobile transformer, which they had in the field yard. Within 24 hours, the vast majority of these isolated areas were powered back up. With Brad's quick thinking and phone calls from Alaska, coupled with immediate decisions and actions from dispatch and all field offices and crews in the three state regions, the nearly impossible was accomplished.

CHAPTER 7 - THE NEXT DAYS AFTER THE BLAST

Rapid City has always been an independent city with independent-minded people, and this turned out to be a great advantage to the newbies from Washington, DC. The outer properties of Rapid City were made into strongholds to keep others from entering the city. And many others went to protect other communities and homes in and around the Black Hills. It didn't start that way, and several gunfights occurred when outsiders entered someone's home. Fortunately, gun ownership was open here for hunting or just target practice, so most homes had a gun or so. Those within the city helped outer neighborhoods, and definite lines were developed between the city and the campers outside the city. However, everyone was an American, so agreements quickly occurred, particularly since the federal government was providing supplies for many communities throughout the areas that still had power. The government knew that these areas would be hit hard by newcomers and was trying to provide assistance.

The civic approach described above was a relief to newly arrived congress personnel, but they wanted more, so many Rapid City residents were hired as guards for both Rapid City metro and the way out to Ellsworth Air Force Base. Within short order, the security for this area had been solidified. But what about other areas in the lower 48 states?

On day one after the blast, the president of the United States was quickly advised to make statements on any media network that he could gain coverage. Unfortunately, communications in the country were still being assessed. The Secretary for the Department of Homeland Security was already on top of this issue and was assisted by the Department of Defense in securing key long-range and powerful AM radio towers. Full-time security was placed 24 hours a day at all locations, and backup generators were being adapted to power. Within the second day after the blast, enough towers were in place to relay the president's message. Here it is in full…

"This message is meant for the American people as well as our good neighbors in Canada and Mexico. The lower 48 States of our Union have experienced an unprovoked attack from Russia. The United States has and is now conducting counterattacks on Russia and Russian-aligned countries, as you are hearing this message. We will continue our missile counterattacks for days to come. They are towards Russia and North Korea. No other country will experience the wrath of the United States unless they are provocative towards us or our allies. We have already gained the upper hand in this near-world conflict, and continued targets will ensure this. Let me be very clear about this. No other attacks on United States property will happen. We know what happened, and best of all, we know what to do to defend our country. Both sides of Congress and both parties of our great country are aligned, and the United States will no longer take any threats from any country. By threats, I mean that we will no longer sit back while any country even suggests attacks on the

United States. We have sat by and allowed Russia and North Korea to make outrageous statements in the past, but that has ended. It has ended, and we are making damn sure of that now.

As for China, we do not anticipate any adverse reaction. We are in constant communication with China now. They have assured us that they will stay out of this conflict.

Now, let me explain the damages. Three nuclear bombs have exploded at 100 miles above the lower 48 states, one above Washington DC, one above Nebraska, and one above California. Thankfully, Alaska and Hawaii are undamaged. One other nuclear blast occurred above London, England, and they are now experiencing what we are, and that is a loss of most of the power grid for the Eastern and Western United States as well as the Texas grid. You are hearing my message because generators are powering radio towers. Please keep your dial to these channels for frequent updates.

The supply chain in the lower 48 states has been broken, and we are making repairs to this system day and night. I ask you and all Americans to be as calm as possible during this exceptional time and help one another if possible. I suggest that neighborhoods create security teams and also team up to provide food, water, fuel, and medicine. Water and food will also be airdropped from both our nearby neighbors of Canada and Mexico, but this will take time, and this is a big country with a lot of need right now. Let's show the world what it means to be an American and to help our brothers and sisters.

It is my obligation to tell you the truth about this situation, and it is that many people will die in our hospitals, senior homes, and locations where food and or water are scarce. It is for this reason that I ask those who can help in these areas to please do so. Also, and this is very important. If you work for security of any kind or the military or National Guard, we need your help immediately. Please secure your home and family first, of course, and then report to your command.

Our rebuilding will be concurrent. It will be communications, power, and fuel. If you work in one of these areas, I ask you to help with the rebuild now. If not, please help secure the families of those who do so that they can get the United States up and running again ASAP.

Your electronic devices may not work and this could be because the satellite or cell tower was damaged or your device was damaged by the blast. It is suggested that you try your device sparingly, saving your battery. Some satellites and cellular towers were damaged, but others were not, given their proximity to the nuclear blast. For instance, if the satellite was on the other side of the earth during the blast, it would be fully functional. If your device is damaged, then get with someone else, and always listen to this AM channel for updates.

To summarize, we in the United States will NOT be attacked again, so we are safe from that. But danger and risk occur everywhere in the lower 48 states due to shortages of food, water, medicine, fuel, and any un-American people that would take advantage of others.

Criminal Types: this message is for you. I have instructed all police and security departments, as well as our military and national guard, to shoot to kill anyone that causes harm to another. Be good to one another.

We will get past this terrible situation, I assure you, and we will come out the other side much stronger and more united.

I will have frequent updates as time continues.

May God bless the United States of America as well as its neighbors and allies."

That message was the first of many from the president and press secretary. The president required that communication with the citizens be continued 24 hours per day and seven days per week, as long as it takes. Someone needs to be repeating this message and updating as more develops, and no recordings. The president thought it would be of some comfort to the American public to have a real person from the federal government continually speaking. These broadcasts did help, but the real-life situation on the ground in the lower 48 states was dire and deadly, depending on where you lived.

After the blast and power was lost in most of the United States, most store workers thought that power would come on in a few minutes. But after having no power or communication for hours, most people went home. It was confusing, to say the least. The bright blasts in the night sky, and then everything goes dark. Store managers eventually locked up and went home, too, and this was done nationwide. Even gas stations were closed. It was an eerie feeling. This situation never happened before. Every previous day was somewhat predictable and even boring. Most people were sleeping during the blast, but the uncertainty of events was starting to take hold.

By early morning after the blast, most people knew something was wrong. It didn't take long for people to realize the risks that everyone was going to experience. Grocery stores were inundated, and everything was taken. Nobody was working, so doors were broken early, and anyone could enter without question. It didn't seem right to just go into the store and take things, but it seemed that everyone was, and everyone wanted to take care of their families with food, water, and security.

Not everyone got the message from the president, but eventually, most did, and for now, desperation had not sunk in. Unfortunately, by nighttime, things began to change rapidly.

Gun stores everywhere in the lower 48 states were ransacked. Everyone knew that the main danger would be others trying to get what you have. Many shootings did occur in most larger cities, and the injured did get some treatment by bystanders. However, nobody was there to take the dead, and this was unsettling.

By the second morning after the blast, the police and military were starting to show up in force. It was like after Pearl Harbor in 1941 when many young people of the time wanted to help defend their country.

The mayors and governors understood the communication deficiencies and would eventually communicate when working satellites and cellular towers were operational, but this would take weeks. It would be a struggle to gain order to larger cities from now on out. But it wasn't just the people in the cities that were worried.

Rural people within the United States started to understand the risks of those coming in from the cities. All small towns sold out of guns and ammo quickly. Nobody wanted a bloodbath, but that was about to happen in some areas, given the desperate times of city people looking for food and water for survival. Here are some examples of difficult events throughout the United States within the first week after the blasts....

New York and large population areas of the eastern seaboard: When power shut down in New York, so did the pumps that kept the subway system dry, so it was not just communications but travel that became difficult in the densely populated parts of New York and other large cities. Elevators were not operational unless some kind of backup power was used, and even then, the backup power was temporary so this meant that the people in high-rise neighborhoods needed to use the stairways to get food and water, so these higher-up residences were difficult and even impossible for the elderly or the disabled.

On the ground level, there was chaos and extreme danger. The New York police department is an army, and power outages are planned for, but not for weeks. Gunfights became common during the days and weeks before some power was resumed. The dead would sometimes lie on the streets until the limited city trucks would show up to load them. With the dead common in the inner city, so was sewage and trash build-up. The city could barely keep up with gathering the dead, so trash just built up, and the stench was everywhere. Disease was a top worry for the mayors of all major cities of the eastern seaboard.

The worst situation in the New York area was a few days after the blast. Although the police had secured much of the area, large gangs still persisted, and on one warm night, about 200 drunk and drugged-up young people became so out of control that they stormed into one of the most elite high-rises in the city. They broke through the front entrance and easily outgunned the first-floor security team. Then, they started walking up the stairs to the residences. Scores of them would enter each of the lower ten floors, shooting up the place and ramming through the door to each apartment. Screams could be heard for blocks as some women were raped and then killed. Then, some bodies of the dead would be dumped over the balcony railing. It was a horror to hear and see the bodies drop to the street below. Everything of value was stolen. Then, the gang members would go up the floors of this 60-floor high-rise and do it all over again until they reached the top floors.

The police were on site within 15 minutes and started going up the high-rise floor by floor. Rapid gunfire was heard for hours as the police tried to take control. As darkness overtook the city, it seemed that the gunfights slowed somewhat. Then, after some moments of silence, more shooting was heard and this went on all night, and on the ground, you could see where the police were by their flashlights and occasional shots ringing out.

The next morning, the shooting stopped, and the city began to collect the bodies of the dead. The police slowly exited the building, and surprisingly, there were no arrests. Every gang member was killed, and nobody questioned this because this was an urban battle with no prisoners.

Chicago and the mid-west to Oklahoma: Generally, the mid-west had a better chance for survival than much of the country. The population was less than the eastern seaboard, other than several large, dense cities, and this area had much more fresh water than the western states. Ranching and farming are abundant here, and August was perfect for gaining newly grown vegetables. Distribution of food was a problem, as it was everywhere, so governors within the mid-west quickly built distribution routes that covered all large and mid-sized cities. This distribution plan left out a large population within smaller cities and towns, but it was the best that could be accomplished. Fortunately, the smaller communities were closer to the farms and ranches, and small militia-type bands were established to transport food to outer regions and communities. Mid-westerners are a special group. Generally, they do help out neighbors, and this is what happened. The Midwest showed what it was to be an American, and after the country healed, many stories of neighbors helping neighbors were told to the world.

Denver and the Front Range Urban Corridor (Cheyenne, Wyoming to Pueblo, Colorado) plus Salt Lake City, Utah from Ogden to Provo: The time of year for this attack to happen was ideal for most of the country, except the west coast. Denver was previously known as cow town decades ago, but these days, it's a party and sports city. Denver is an all-pro city with all-American professional teams, and most of them play at stadiums in the downtown area. It is for this reason that the population of downtown neighborhoods has been growing fast. High-rise apartments and condominium homes are frequently built due to this high demand in the RiNo neighborhood as well as LoDo and the Golden Triangle, and also up Welton Street towards Five-Points. Actually, many neighborhoods all over the metro are growing faster than ever before, and this is due to reasonable weather with lots of sunshine and, of course, the many activities in the mountains.

The people of Denver are mainly from nearby states of Wyoming, South Dakota, Nebraska, Kansas, and New Mexico, so Denver and Colorado, in general, have a mixture of people from smaller communities looking for employment or the excitement of this fun city with nearby activities of skiing and hiking. It was these people that made this location more survivable than other large population areas.

When the blasts occurred, this area was still in the hot season but cooling off at night. The nearly regular rain storms were still occurring between 2 and 4 pm, so clean water was available after the city water supply dried up. Food was more challenging, though, and when store-bought foods were being depleted, many would make hunting trips into the mountains or surrounding prairies, and this caused problems. With about 3 ½ million residents in the Denver metro area, this meant a lot of hunters trying for the same game. Within weeks of the blast, the hunting was reasonably safe, but as time continued, more desperation surfaced and this caused anger, and gun fights started, so many went further out from the city. Unfortunately, trouble occurred when someone was transporting their kill back home. It was for this reason that gangs or small militias were developed, and even then, battles would often take place. Eventually, a dominant group (or small army) would prevail, and borders were developed. These groups would do anything necessary to gain food and then transport the food back to the city for sale to the highest bidder, cash only.

Airdrops of food were becoming more regular from Mexico, and this helped stabilize the surviving population, but only after thousands of people in this area had died due to hunger, violence, or lack of local medicine and healthcare.

The Salt Lake City metropolitan area from Ogden to Provo experienced similarities to the Front Range of

Colorado but less gang activity. Water was not as much of an issue here because of all of the freshwater lakes in the mountains. The Great Salt Lake was an option for water as well, but the salt would obviously need to be removed first. Distillation was the best method for this water. It is fortunate that such a large metropolitan area is stretched along the mountains rather than concentrating in one area. This metro layout was a great advantage for people heading to the mountains for food or water. Generally speaking, this area was better off than most of the country.

Minneapolis and Saint Paul Metropolitan Area: The Minneapolis and Saint Paul metro area, as well as all of Minnesota and the lake areas of South Dakota, fared much better. Here, fresh water is of no issue, and fishing is abundantly available. The fall season is the best here as well, making this the best time for a disaster of this type. Winter cold was a few months off, and the people of this northern area were accustomed to planning and staying on top of winter chores. The rural areas were much more prepared than city folk, of course, but many from the city have roots in other areas outside of the city. The inner city had terrible issues with the high-rises downtown, and the downtown population was sizable. Most deaths occurred in the inner-city areas of Minneapolis and Saint Paul.

Florida and Southern States: This area of the country was, without doubt, the best place to be outside of Alaska and Hawaii. Florida has three sides of coastline, and other southern states border the Gulf of Mexico and this was perfect for all seafood types. It was salt water, but freshwater rain occurred regularly, and the distilling of salt water was also a good option. Fresh seafood was more plentiful here than anywhere else in the country. The population was huge, and gangs were everywhere, but desperation was less prevalent here, and survival was much better, with the exception of the high-rise neighborhoods. As with all other places in the United States, cash was king. For some reason, many people here had stashes of cash, which made trading more real than most other areas.

The most destructive occurrence in Florida was in Miami. Miami has always been a party town, and on one particularly hot evening, the locals crowded into the streets, many drunk and partying. It didn't take long for anger to happen, and guns were drawn. Shots were everywhere, and this caused more panic and others to pull out weapons. It was shoot or be shot for those who didn't escape the streets that night. Police had no chance to stop this as it went on for many blocks in the downtown areas and nearby beaches. The only good thing is that the shooting was over after about four hours. In the morning, several hundred people lie on the ground dead or dying, and it is only at this time that the police had any chance of regaining control.

Texas - Dallas, Fort Worth, Houston, Austin, San Antonio: Texas is mentioned as a separate location because it's a huge state and it also has its own power grid. It is obvious that the lone-star-state wanted to maintain some level of independence ever since it became a part of the United States, and this turned out to be an advantage of sorts. The large cities experienced issues similar to those in Denver, but

Texas also had a coastline, and this made seafood more available. Ranching is big in Texas, so fresh meat was occasionally distributed after bartering with the state governor and mayors. Refrigeration was extremely uncommon after the blasts, so any butchering of animals occurred just before transporting. The governor made sure that the limited distribution of fuel went to the food delivery caravans with a heavy escort.

The Houston area was particularly hit hard after the first couple of weeks since the blast. The heat and humidity made things so uncomfortable, and the lack of food made things worse. Large areas of downtown and nearby neighborhoods expressed their anger with gun fights and fist fights. Police were sparse in many areas, and they had no chance of getting things controlled, so this went on for days until the National Guard was organized and brought in.

Phoenix and Tucson: This area was next to the worst area to be in during this situation. Water in this area is extremely scarce, and food wasn't much better. Leaving these large cities would mean going into the hot desert, but there are places reasonably close to these cities that are higher in elevation and, therefore, cooler in the summer, as in 90's vs 100's. Prescott, Sedona, Cottonwood, and Flagstaff were destinations out of the big cities. Not only were they a little cooler, they typically got more rainfall, and water was the biggest issue for everyone. Gang activity was a little worse than in northern cities but better than in Southern California. In either case, lawlessness occurred in all downtown areas.

Rain does occur here more than in Southern California at this time of the year. Unfortunately, this area did not offer much relief, and death in this area of Arizona was from a lack of good, clean drinking water. For those who made it up to Flagstaff, the situation was better, and the lower population helped.

Las Vegas: Las Vegas has had nearly steady growth since the 1960's, when it was a much smaller town. Fortunately for those in this city, they had the large desert lakes to go to, such as Lake Mead and Lake Mohave. Both of these lakes have been going down in water reserves, but they are huge lakes and still offer a lot of lakefront to camp at and have fresh water to distill or boil for drinking.

Los Angeles and Southern California: This was the worst time for this attack to happen, and Southern California was the worst place to be. The hottest time of the year here is between August and early winter when the Santa Anna winds blow from the deserts to the cool ocean. This time period is typically looked at as summer for this area of the country. To make matters worse, the population here is huge and spread out.

Normally, this area is mostly relaxed, except for freeway driving, so when the blast occurred, it didn't take effect on most of the population. However, within a day of not getting gas for the car or a beer for the evening, things changed rapidly, and it occurred first in the hotter eastern and central suburbs. Gang activity in this part of the country is common but controlled. However, when police and security broke down during the first couple of days after the blast, lawlessness became the norm. It was too hot to go inland, so the coast was the natural progression of this enormous population. Of course, the richer people lived in this cooler area of Southern California, and that would be the demise of those living there. Water was the main issue because animals would die of thirst before starvation, and most people know it doesn't rain in Southern California from about April until about October.

Almost everyone in this area had enough fuel to drive across town to the ocean, and millions did. To nobody's surprise, there was a massive traffic jam, but walking that distance was also doable.

The residents in Malibu and all coastal cities were not anywhere close to prepared for protecting themselves. It was a bloodbath. Gang members easily overtook any resistance and established their headquarters in mansions overlooking the beautiful Pacific Ocean. This was one area of the country that was not going to be rebuilt until much after control was gained in the rest of the United States.

Bay Area of California plus Sacramento, Stockton, and Tracy: Unlike Southern California, Northern California was better. Rain also doesn't happen from about April to October, but the Marine Layer (high-level fog) covers the coastal areas, and the Delta offers reasonable fresh water. Fishing occurs throughout the San Francisco Bay, the huge Delta region, and both the Scarcement River and San

Joaquin River. Drinkable water and a food source were much more available than in the southern part of California.

However, the problem was the population, as well as in other areas of the country. Over 8 million people live in this area, and panic can change everything.

This metropolitan area is traversed by many freeways connected to bridges. In order to control mass migrations, the highway patrol closed all bridges, with the exception of emergencies. This action saved San Francisco and the peninsula that it's on. About a million or so people live on the peninsula, and the only land mass connecting to it is from the south (San Jose area). For this reason, this metro area became one of the safest cities in the country. Saltwater is on three sides, and companies started to distill this seawater into fresh water for a price. Also, fishing occurred on these three sides, so many fishing boats (if they had fuel) could make a fortune selling to this hungry population. The end results showed that fewer people died here from starvation or thirst.

San Jose to Oakland to Sacramento didn't fare so well, but they also had better access to fresh water and food sources. The growing fields in this area are some of the best in the world.

The Northwest from Portland to Seattle: Many people view Washington State and Oregon State as similar, and they'd be right. Both have coastlines with good fishing and mountain areas for other wild game. As with all other areas in the United States, the rural areas fared much better than the cities.

Unfortunately, in Seattle and Portland, they already had a large homeless population. This homeless population made things much worse due to this already desperate population. High-rise neighborhoods bartered with some homeless to supply food and water to all floors of these tall residential buildings. In return, they kept some food and water and were given places in buildings to get off of the streets at night. As you might imagine, drug addicts didn't turn out to be good workers and many homeless were not strong enough for this type of work either. It may seem inhumane to ignore these people, but these were desperate times. Only the homeless who could work were given the advantages of food, water, and some safety off of the street. Just as in New York and other large cities, the mayor had trucks picking up the dead. Disease was always a concern. For those who died, the city tried to gather as much information about them as possible prior to burying them in mass graves. The best advantage that Seattle and Portland had was the shipping lanes from other countries that were not affected by the blasts. For this reason, supplies were coming in fast, and this included food, water, and fuel.

Many people traveled to Canada to find safer areas. Fortunately, north of here, things improved.

CHAPTER 8 – TROUBLE IN LUSK, WYOMING

When Brad went to his office, he could see the signs of the previous day's work. As mentioned earlier large paper maps were on every tabled surface, with writing and drawings made with a red sharpy pen. Brad could see the effort and logic in establishing the isolation boundaries. His boss was there, and it was obvious that he was camping out there as well. All of his coworkers were out at various substations, camping there most nights in order to ensure things worked, and they did. The boss assigned every person in his group to an area to keep secure. They were to spend nights there if necessary and to report any problems to the field office, and that explained why the boss was living in the office. Brad was assigned a large area from Torrington, Wyoming, up to Mule Creek Junction and from Old Woman Creek to Interstate 25. This area was big in milage, but Brad knew it well. He stayed in Lusk, Wyoming, at his favorite Best Western Motel. This place wasn't fancy, but it was well-maintained and clean. It also had free breakfast in the morning featuring the best pork green chili he ever had, equal to the best restaurants in Denver, Colorado, which is famous for Colorado green chili.

Brad let Ella know his plans and packed up for several nights. As he was walking out the door to his work truck, Ella yelled, "Take your gun with you." Brad hadn't thought of it, but given the situation, he walked back to get his Colt 45 revolver. It was his favorite gun, a second-generation, single-action revolver made in 1957, an exact replica of the first-generation Colt 45. He grabbed a box of bullets, and then he was off. On his way out, he stopped at his neighbor's house, which had the CB and Ham radio (TJ). TJ gave Brad his contact handle name and told him what channels he monitored. After that, Brad was on the road toward Lusk.

It was great to be in Lusk at this time of the year. Tourist season would normally be ending, but not this year. Many tourists were stuck and couldn't get back home, so they stayed in hotels if they could afford it, or they stayed in parks. In Lusk, there were about 30 people stuck there. The locals helped them with food and water and even arranged for the local school gymnasium so they could stay out of the weather. A few could afford motels, and Brad met many of them while he stayed in Lusk.

The reason that Brad was assigned to this area was because the transformer for the town was one of the transformers that was damaged during the blast, and his boss wanted his best man in this location. From this location, Brad could easily visit all substations in this area, including larger substations in Torrington, Wheatland, and Douglas, Wyoming. All of these locations were well maintained, and since the weather was cooling down, energy demand was going down, so all was okay.

Several days had passed since the blast, and bad news was being reported from Denver and other large cities in the entire country. Brad listened religiously to AM radio for messages or any broadcasts. He felt good about being where he was, knowing that the lower population, as well as the independence of the people, made this the ideal place to be. But Brad didn't anticipate the desperation of people in Denver, and he certainly didn't understand the gang mentality regarding money and power. Towards the end of the first week after the blast, a caravan of vehicles left Denver, heading north. The people in this group had heard that electricity was available in eastern Wyoming, so this group of seven men and four women traveled in four vehicles up Interstate 25 toward Cheyenne, Wyoming. They had two camper vans and two pickup trucks. They stole about 150 gallons of gas from nearby vehicles in order to get far enough up into Wyoming, thinking that gas stations would still be operating there. Their goal was simple: to steal as much money and sellable goods as possible to get rich, and they didn't care if they needed to kill to get it. The way they figured was that this was their one chance to get big money because of the dysfunction of society and organized police officers.

They could only guess, but they were somewhat correct. Even the Governor of Wyoming was looking for more security, and he invited an old friend of his to be part of his security detail. This person was the police chief of Lusk, and he didn't want to leave his community with only one police officer. But the Governor insisted, saying that Lusk was too far north for any looters, and the town had another officer in town and also good, solid people who would help out if needed. The police chief eventually had to go, though, or he knew he would never get help from the Governor for anything in the future. He was currently asking the Governor for extra funding for an upgraded emergency vehicle, and the Governor hinted that this vehicle could be on the next budget if the police chief headed the security detail for just one month.

The caravan from Denver traveled up the freeways and past Longmont, Loveland, and Fort Collins. The scene was weird because of the many vehicles that ran out of gas and were abandoned on the interstate. Anyway, this caravan made it through Cheyenne with no problems. Cheyenne was also experiencing a power outage, just like most of the country. Once past Cheyenne, they got off of the interstate in the hope of finding a reasonably small community to steal from. They assumed that small communities depended on a county sheriff for police protection, and so they were not interested in larger towns. Also, they wanted to find a small town that was far from other towns where the police could help. As they traveled northeast, they noticed signs of the town of Torrington, and they thought that this would be perfect. They were disappointed, though, when they saw how big it was. This place surely had a police department, so they continued going north. The next town was Lingle, but it was too small and would not have enough money or sellable goods to steal. Then they came across what they viewed as a sleepy small town that was big enough to have a good amount of cash. This town was clean and well-kept and even had some static displays of old cars and farm equipment for aesthetics. This situation was perfect; any town that is this well-kept certainly has some money in it. The town was Lusk, Wyoming.

It was late in the evening, so they decided to get one hotel room for the night for the shower and toilet, but most of them would sleep in the camper vans. They stayed at the Best Western, the very same place that Brad was staying, and Brad was getting to the motel just as they were checking in. Brad noticed them first thing because something just wasn't right about this group. He noticed the Colorado license plates (greenies, as they call them in Wyoming). Brad noticed that they were not a family group, so he was a little suspicious. But these were not normal times, so he pushed it out of his mind and settled in for the evening.

That night was alarming. This Colorado group was getting drunk in the room next to his, and Brad could make out a few words of what they were saying. It appeared that a couple of the lead guys were disagreeing on how to rob people and businesses. At about midnight, they went to sleep, and Brad didn't feel that he had enough information enough to call the police that night.

It was hard to sleep that night, but Brad got a couple of hours before he was up for the day. The room next to his was quiet, and so were the camper vans parked nearby. Brad got his breakfast made up of a breakfast burrito smothered in delicious green chili sauce, and then he was on the road. But before he went too far, he stopped by the police station to warn them of the suspicious conversation he heard the night before.

Brad started his day in Torrington, checking the equipment in the substation. His plan was to check on various equipment while working his way back to Lusk by evening. He was in Lingle by lunch at Lira's restaurant and noticed a flickering in the lights, so he used his radio to contact dispatch. They said that something was happening at the Lusk temporary transformer, so Brad jumped in his truck and sped off to Lusk, about a half hour away. When he arrived, he saw the two camper vans parked next to the substation. Brad parked a short distance away and saw a couple of people in the substation yard. Brad yelled at them to get out and said that it was private property. At that, about six people came into view, and most of them had guns. One pointed his gun at Brad and told him to "get fucking lost." Brad was out-gunned, so this was one of the absolute times to retreat and call up reinforcements.

Brad called the police on his radio, and only one officer was available. The chief of police was temporarily assigned to help secure the Governor, and that left one remaining officer, who quickly met up with Brad at a safe location about two blocks from the substation. There was no way that the two of them could take on these guys, so they tried to contact the Torrington police department. Unfortunately, cell phones were unreliable due to damage done to cell towers and satellites.

Lusk, Wyoming

Lusk Substation

CHAPTER 9 – GANGS vs LOCALS, LINEMAN and the LAW

Brad and the one remaining law officer looked out from behind a small building at the transmission yard where the gang members parked their camper vans. It was easily seen that six people were trying to decide how to shut the transformer down. They didn't plan this very well, but they knew that they had to shut it down so that the other five gang members could start robbing the stores in the downtown area, starting with a very busy gas station that obviously had good business.

Brad knew they could not take on this gang with just the two of them, and Brad had previously counted 11 people in this Colorado group. Brad thought about it for a minute and then had an idea. He would call TJ in Gillette from his truck radio and ask him to run over to Terry's house to see if Terry and a friend or two could drive down to Lusk for backup. Brad didn't know anyone in Lusk, but he knew Terry would help. Brad said one more thing to TJ, and that was to let Terry know that there was going to be a gunfight with 11 gang members from Colorado who were trying to rob the town. TJ took the message and immediately ran over to Terry's house.

The police officer had another idea about getting help. He knew a couple of guys who worked in a small bar across Main Street from the Best Western. The police vehicle also had an emergency radio, so they agreed on a channel, and the police officer took off for the bar. Brad stayed to see if he could do anything to stop the gang from taking the transformer down.

The temporary mobile transformer had several conductors connecting it to the substation. The blown transformer was still in place but completely disconnected from the substation. It was these conductors that the gang members were looking at. One guy grabbed a large wrench of some kind, thinking he could undo the bolted conductor lead, but when he touched the wrench to the bolt, he received another kind of bolt; a bolt of electricity hit him immediately, and his gang friends watched his body torque until he fell flat on the ground dead. This sudden death shocked the shit out of the remaining gang members, and after about a minute, they all pulled out weapons and started to shoot at the transformer. It didn't take long before the temporary mobile transformer crackled and then burst into flames. The gang lost a member but was successful in shutting the transformer down. To Brad's surprise, the five gang members left the body of their supposed friend and drove the camper vans out of the substation yard towards downtown.

Brad watched the vehicles leave and then followed them until they parked in a parking lot near a grocery store. All of these events took about 20 minutes in total. Brad was still out of sight when his boss called him on the emergency radio, asking what was going on with the Lusk substation. Brad brought his boss up to speed and then asked him if he could contact the Wyoming Highway Patrol. Then Brad called the police officer, who agreed to meet up at 4th and Elm

Street, just one block over from the grocery parking lot.

It had now been about 40 minutes since Brad contacted TJ in Gillette, and Terry and four of his friends were speeding down State Highway 59. They were all on their Harleys because when TJ informed them of Brad's request, they were just bullshitting and working on one of the bikes, and also, they get better gas mileage than cars and trucks. Typically, the trip between Gillette and Lusk would be 2 ½ hours, but they didn't have much traffic and gunned the throttle, practically flying down the highway.

The police officer and two local cowboys got out of the police vehicle and joined Brad in his double cab truck. Brad explained about the transformer and where these five gang members parked. Brad said he had reinforcements coming in from Gillette, but it would take time for them to travel. They all knew that they could not wait too long or someone might get killed, so they decided to split up in groups of two and walk over to Main Street and then slowly walk north to downtown from there, cautiously observing the situation.

By the time they were in position on both sides of Main Street, near the grocery store, it had been 50 minutes. At their positions, they could see that the convenience store had already been robbed, and the ten remaining gang members were splitting up, five on either side of Main Street, presumably to rob stores as they walked north on Main Street.

Meanwhile, Terry and his friends had earlier sped past the tiny town of Bill, Wyoming.

Little did the gang know that Brad, the officer, and two local cowboys (carrying newer Colt 45 revolvers) were approaching them from the south.

The gang noticed a bank that was one block north of the convenience store that they just shot up, and Brad could see them hastily planning the bank robbery. It took them some time, but eventually, five gang members went to the bank, leaving the other five across the street, waiting for a shootout if necessary. The next thing Brad heard was rapid gunfire from within the bank.

Brad knew it was now or never if they wanted to stop this gang from hurting or killing the local folks downtown. Brad was in a good range of the five gang members, so he aimed his pistol and pulled the trigger. One gang member fell to the ground in pain, while the other 4 turned their attention to Brad and the officer next to him. Everyone took cover, including the two local cowboys on the east side of Main Street. The gang had a couple of fully automatic weapons, so they sprayed bullets in the direction of Brad and the officer. The cowboys across the street had a Winchester rifle and two Colt 45 revolvers. One guy aimed the Winchester and got a shot off at the gang before they noticed them. The shot was right on, and the gang member fell to the street, moved a little, and then went still. He died quickly. At this, the one remaining automatic weapon was shot in the direction of the cowboys, and one was hit in the shoulder and in pain. The other cowboy helped his friend around the corner of the building and out of gunshot range. He stopped the bleeding by plugging the bullet hole with fabric and then used another piece of fabric to cover the area before tightly wrapping the shoulder in duct tape that was provided by the many downtown merchants who were taking shelter but arming themselves as well.

The shooting stopped for a few minutes as both sides of this fight found better cover and reloaded. Brad assumed ten gang members were downtown, given one of the original eleven died at the substation. Two of these were out of commission, one dead, and one badly injured. That left eight, five in the bank and three plus the wounded guy, hiding in the drug store building across Main Street from the bank. Brad asked the officer to guard the back of the drug store while he positioned himself to get a shot if someone came out of either the drug store or the bank. The uninjured cowboy was back on Main Street after helping his friend. Other locals took care of his friend, freeing him up to backup Brad. They were badly outgunned, and the only reason that the gang didn't rush them was that they didn't know it was only three guys advancing on them (a police officer, Brad, and the uninjured cowboy). Other locals were arming themselves and taking defensive positions in case the gang went into other stores.

Brad had a good shot of the bank entrance, and the local cowboy had a good shot of the front entrance to the drugstore. This situation worked out nicely, at least for the moment. But that's when all hell broke loose, and several gang members charged into the street with guns blazing. Both Brad and the cowboy were hit, and both were stuck in doorways in neighboring buildings. Brad was hit in the shoulder, and the cowboy was hit in his upper arm. Brad and the cowboy got a couple of shots off, and they hit their intended targets. It was risky for the gang to do this, but they gained an advantage by doing it. The gang had all 4 of their vehicles parked on the street, and 4 of them ran out to start them for a quick escape. The injuries that both Brad and the cowboy were not immediately life-threatening, but they were enough to keep them from making any further advancements and this created the perfect opportunity for the gang to escape. It did, that is until the thunder of five bikers from Gillette showed up. They had just arrived in town from the west and traveled north towards downtown. They stopped on the street near the shot-up convenience store while several local people ran out to them to explain the situation.

Knowing the situation, Terry and the others pulled out pistols in their left hands and gunned the gas with their right hand. As they rode towards the gang's vehicles, they pointed the guns at the drivers and drove past while firing the guns. This sudden driveby shocked the crap out of the gang members, and they tried to regroup back in the bank and drug store. Terry and his friends parked in an out-of-sight parking area, and they all approached Main Street on the north side of the drug store and bank. They surrounded the gang on all sides. The officer guarded the back door to the drug store while other locals took up position at the back of the bank, and Brad and the cowboy, although both injured, were positioned on Main Street, south of the drug store and bank.

It was a standoff for about 10 minutes while both sides of this battle repositioned themselves to what they thought were better positions. That's when one of the local women yelled, "Come on out, you fucking cowards." She was a well-respected citizen of Lusk, a church-going lady in her 70s. Another local lady started in by yelling, "You're a bunch of chicken shits." This lady's opinion opened the Pandora's box for the local men and women of all ages and backgrounds to taunt these gang members with many insults. It was funny coming from decent people that were just fed up with crime, and damn it, they were not going to take it. Terry and his friends had a good laugh at this, knowing the people in Gillette would not take this kind of shit either.

Within a minute of the insult-slinging, the gang members had coordinated a rush for the vehicles. They had signaled each other from the windows for their escape. Given the crossfire could hit the wrong target, few shots were fired, but two gang members did get hit and fell to the ground as the remaining gang took off in the vehicles traveling north. Terry and his friends were not going to allow this, so they shot up the driver's side as the gang tried to drive past. None of the vehicles made it, and all went off the road before reaching a large bridge over a railroad track. The remaining gang members were not going to give up and exited the vehicles, only to be chased down by locals and shot or captured.

The highway patrol drove into town just after this happened and took the living gang members into custody. All-in-all three gang members survived with injuries, and the others died. Brad and six locals had gunshot injuries, including the cowboy helping Brad, three in the bank, and two others in the corner convenience store. They all were treated and would make full recoveries.

The story of the Lusk shootout would spread like wildfire through this area of the state and in South Dakota, too.

It was a short celebration in Lusk because the town's power was out again, one time by the Russians and one more time by the Denver outlaw gang. Brad was responsible for this area, so he tried everything he knew to get another compatible transformer. Then, out of the blue, he was contacted by TJ in Gillette. TJ was contacted by another emergency radio operator in Rapid City, and he had good news. It seemed that a well-known power contractor in Rapid City had heard of the transformer going out again in Lusk, and they had a mobile transformer that might work. The construction company was named Blink Construction, and that is where Brad started his career. They saw something in him when he was young and hired him when jobs were hard to find. Brad spent ten years at Blink before being offered a job package and a job position that he couldn't turn down. It was hard to leave Blink Construction, but everyone understood, given the offer he was given. Brad had already had the reputation of someone who gets the job done, and hence this job offer. He didn't want to leave Rapid, but he liked Gillette and where it was located, between the Black Hills and the Rocky Mountains.

Brad knew about the thick coal deposit under Gillette and thought that if he could buy some land above this layer with mineral rights, he might be able to make some real money. The downturn in coal usage didn't damper his dreams about this. To him, coal is stored energy, and eventually, it would be of great value someday, although he jokingly said it would probably happen after he died. Brad had about 100 acres of land plus his house in town at the time of the blast.

Blink Construction offered free rental of this mobile transformer plus free delivery and installation and this was completed within a couple of days of the "Lusk Shootout", which it was being termed by the media.

The Governor made a special trip to Lusk a day after the shootout, and he released the Lusk chief of police from his security detail so that he could go back to his job and help with the rebuild. The Governor also promised federal and/or state aid to the shot-up buildings and healthcare costs for those who were injured. Then, the Governor left kind of fast because he knew the residents of Lusk were not happy that he took their chief of police away from them just before their time of need. He really was a good governor of the state.

After Lusk had their second transformer installed, Brad spent more time in Gillette with Ella and friends.

CHAPTER 10 – RELOCATED GOVERNMENT

The relocation of the United States government has had pre-emptive planning to known destinations, but to relocate immediately to an unplanned area was a first. Fortunately, Ellsworth is a good-sized Air Force Base and is near Rapid City, with a modern regional airport that has direct flights to many large cities in the country.

Ellsworth Air Force base was immediately put on alert for many upcoming aircraft landings, and the flights started coming in within an hour of the government's realization that power was still on in this area. The president was airborne at this time, and the vice president went to an undisclosed backup located underground. Long-term power was anticipated for this underground bunker, and the president and vice president were always aware of the other's situation.

The original mission for this Air Force base was now secondary to the relocation of the president and Congress. Every available room and space was being planned for something. The Pine Tree Inn became the permanent location for the presidency staff, and the president was located in a secretive nearby building, but everyone on base knew where he was staying. Congress created office space in gyms, cafeterias, and even hangar space. One of the hardest things was finding a place to park the incoming aircraft and keep the runway clear. For this reason, the nearby Rapid City Regional Airport became a high-security location for aircraft and some of the staff for Congress. So many people and supplies were coming into this area that all hotels, motels, and even bed and breakfasts were contracted for incoming government personnel.

 It was a chaotic mess of two full branches of government relocating to western South Dakota. The third branch of government (the Supreme Court) had its own protocol for an emergency event, and that information went blank immediately.

The CIA and FBI also relocated staff for necessary protections, and this was when it was learned of an FBI agent in Denver who was raised in Rapid City and knew the area well. His name was Chris, and he was brought in as the up-front man for the security of Rapid City and Ellsworth Air Force Base. Chris was assigned a two-bedroom apartment in a newly constructed high-rise downtown. This apartment was to be his residence and office because he was now expected to be available 24 hours per day, every day. Chris requested this location because it was close to the ten-floor Alex Johnson Hotel, which would house other security personnel, including forty FBI agents he had worked with previously. Also, the Rapid City police department was within walking distance of his location, and downtown had several good routes to get to Ellsworth Air Force Base quickly.

As mentioned earlier, Chris grew up in Rapid City and graduated from high school and college there. Chris was a widower, but his deceased wife (Ann) was also from Rapid City. Chris also knew two Rapid City police officers since they were kids because Ann helped these two out after their folks were killed in a car accident. The two officers were Maka and her brother Chaiton, and since Chris already knew them, he asked that they be the interface personnel between the FBI and all police and security groups (sheriff, highway patrol, other police in the Black Hills, security police on base, and of course the Rapid City police department.

A physical barrier is already in place around Ellsworth AFB, but not anywhere else. For this reason, Chris set up security entrances on all roads and streets going into Rapid City. It was no secret that many people were trying to get to this area of the country due to the power being on there, but Chris could not allow visitors to enter either Rapid City or Ellsworth AFB. Even the interstate between these two locations would need heavy security.

A perimeter layout was established, and Chris knew he needed about fifty local people to hire as patrol personnel. The FBI Headquarters gave Chris a blank check to secure things, so Chris began a hiring program for anyone who was proven reliable and trustworthy and could handle a gun. Fortunately, that describes a lot of people in the Black Hills area, and within a week, he had most of the people with assigned patrol areas and a 24-hour schedule for shift changes. This scheduling was a massive undertaking, and every person was vetted as best as possible, given the communication obstacles. Chris even set up an emergency human resource group that would modify the staff and schedule as needed, and this freed Chris up for emergency situations that he knew would occur.

The best personnel that Chris would hire would be the escorts to and from Ellsworth Air Force Base, so Chris was always looking for people he could trust. Within a week or so of the blast, Chris had heard of a shootout in nearby Lusk, Wyoming, and it sounded like a group of locals organized to take on a tough gang from Denver. Chris also learned of an emergency radio operator who had contact with other regional radio operators. Chris quickly put the emergency radio operators on his payroll to help with United States communications and tried to hire Brad Zimberman from a federal power company. But Brad's boss said no way because Brad needed to keep the power on. Chris understood but insisted because Brad was a federal employee, and the Lusk Transformer was replaced (again). Reluctantly, Brad's boss allowed him to help out in Rapid. Chris then asked about the five bikers (including Terry) who helped Brad, and he was put in contact with them. A deal was made, and a few box trucks were sent to Gillette to pick up the five men with their supplies and motorcycles. The motorcycles were perfect for tight spaces and maneuverability. Chris found that a couple of these guys were veterans and that all were the kind of people who would help you if needed. He also heard that these guys are not the kind to piss off, and what happened in Lusk, Wyoming, proved that. It was these five men that enabled Chris to hire fifty more bikers, which could be counted on. This hiring solved the security escort issue for the most part. Several Congress personnel expressed concern when they had security motorcycle escorts with long hair, beards and were riding Harley Davidson motorcycles, but after a while, they got used to it, given that Sturgis is just 30 miles away.

Terry became the supervisor for his security escort group and would report directly to Chris on assignments. Terry was an experienced foreman at the coal company where he worked in Gillette. He also supervised the security team at the coal company. You might not think that a security team is needed at a coal company, but Terry personally witnessed three times that people would sneak into the coal yard and shovel coal into a pickup. On one of those occasions, the person brought his own small wheel loader to help him load his truck more quickly. The company didn't prosecute any of these times, though, because they knew anyone doing this was somewhat poor and or disparate.

Brad was assigned the job of securing the border of Rapid City and the Interstate to Ellsworth AFB. Chris thought Brad would be best for this job because of the 50 locals he hired for security, and Brad was originally from Rapid City. Brad had his security clearance in place for many years due to his access requirements to secure locations of the federal power grid system. Brad also has supervisory skills, as he manages others in his group at work.

Chris also knew a couple from Hill City, South Dakota, Ryan and Ann. They were both financially well off due to some exploration when Chris met them a few years ago. Chris knew them both well and trusted them as much as he trusted Maka and Chaiton; in fact, all of them knew each other from difficult times in the past, and Ryan and Ann were previously contract employees of the FBI through Chris during his first assignment with the FBI in South Dakota some time back. He knew that Ryan, Brad, and Terry also knew one another from high school and thought this was the exact group of people he needed to supplement his FBI team. All of them already had security clearances except for Terry. Terry received his security clearance along with the other bikers and people that he hired. It was a quick security clearance process due to the lack of time.

There were many different security groups now in this area. Chris (FBI) included the local escort security team under Terry and the border security team under Brad. Of course, the Air Force base had its security force, but the CIA was also on base. In the city, there was the Rapid City police department and other police departments from towns in the metro area. The county had the sheriff's office, and the state had the highway patrol. Maka and Chaiton worked hand-in-hand with the local and state enforcement groups, and they coordinated with the base and CIA, but this was a lot to deal with, and he needed Ryan and Ann to help specifically with the president and his family.

Ryan and Ann were perfect for this because they already had good reputations with the local and regional forces, and Chris would help get them both involved with the base enforcement because he wanted them to work directly with the president and the president's family. For instance, if the president needed to leave the base for any reason, Ryan and Ann would accompany them as representatives for Chris's group and ride along with the Secret Service.

Ryan was a naturally likable guy in a rougher kind of way, and Ann was smart and caring, and it didn't hurt that Ann was a beautiful lady. Anyway, whenever there was a meeting on base, it would be Chris and a couple of his FBI supervisors, plus Ryan and Ann, and sometimes Terry, if the subject was about transporting someone. If a meeting was in town, then Maka and Chaiton would also attend.

CHAPTER 11 – TYPICAL BORDER ISSUES

The population outside of the border with Rapid City was getting bigger, and more people were showing up for food or medical help. It was a city surrounding a city on all sides. The FBI, in coordination with Brad, had their hands full in trying to secure such a large area as well as the interstate between Rapid and the base. Brad had close to a hundred people working for him now and built teams with one of his friends leading each team and reporting to him. About half were bikers, or people he knew who owned Harley-Davidsons, and the other half were good people from Rapid or other areas in or around the Black Hills. Brad did not know everyone hired, but trusted his friends/supervisors to handle any personnel issues. He needed people to secure the border, but not too aggressively, so this was one of the biggest challenges.

Brad set the teams up with at least one entrance into the city per team. The entrances would have entry stops in which all vehicles were questioned when coming into the city. Anyone could leave the city anytime; it was just entering that was monitored. Monitoring was reasonably straightforward. If a vehicle wanted to enter the city, they needed proof of being a resident or having an immediate medical emergency. There was a lot of leeway and discretion in who would make it into the city, but it worked well. If someone made it into the city that wasn't supposed to be, they would most likely be seen as homeless on the streets. The city police would then pick them up and hand them over to Brad's group, and Brad's group would take them to the city border. This effort took care of the roads in and out of Rapid City, but property between entry stops was not monitored and this became the biggest problem because non-residents could simply walk into the city. The local residents would inform Brad's groups if they had some kind of communication, but otherwise, they defended their own property as they thought necessary, and there were many problems, including fights and even shootings. Brad always sided with the city residents, so this was passed on by word of mouth, which lessened the number coming across the border each night, but every night, there was some activity.

Chris was fully aware of this, and that's why the federal government supplied so much food, water, supplies, and even port-o-pots to those living outside the city. It was always a mess, but Brad did what he could to keep everyone safe. Fortunately, the weather was great at this time of year, so living outside of the city was not hard. After about a week, everyone seemed to understand the process, and skirmishes were happening less often.

The Interstate between Rapid and the base is about fourteen miles, and Brad was also assigned to secure this route for the constant trips by federal personnel. Brad had difficulty figuring this out, so he placed a guard every mile on both sides of the interstate. Each location had a recreational vehicle or some kind of shelter, and each person had an emergency radio or other walkie-talkie to communicate. Everyone was armed with their own weapons, and a second person was also there if they had enough people to divvy out. Of course, shifts were arranged on either 8 hours or 12 hours, depending on how many people were available. Brad checked on these guard locations daily.

In support of checkpoints in the city and on the interstate, Brad created a control facility that was in constant contact with all checkpoints. He also had a quick deployment group that could hit the road anytime. Most of these guys were ex-military and drove whatever they owned, about half Harley and half pickup trucks. These people were the last line of defense that Brad had ready, and they worked twelve-hour shifts, about five per shift. Brad realized that this was not enough, but he could also count on local law enforcement. However, he was always looking for more people, and Chris always backed him with finances.

CHAPTER 12 – ASSULT ON THE CITY

The president and his cabinet worked and lived on Ellsworth AFB, but they took advantage of the Monument Civic Center facility in Rapid City when bigger venues were needed. The Summit Arena is the newest of several large arenas that were once named the Rushmore Plaza Civic Center, and it has brought in large rock and roll bands and other large musical and sports venues. Elvis even played here shortly before he died. This building is used today for Rapid City's hockey and arena football teams. But now, the government regularly uses stadiums of different sizes in the facility to make speeches and hold large meetings. One large speech was going to take place soon, and the rumor was that the president would talk about updates to the country.

All security departments knew the president's agenda, and Terry was planning transportation from Ellsworth to the Monument arena. Ann and Ryan were naturally a part of this because they would accompany the president and staff to and from Ellsworth, along with the Secret Service. Chris and the FBI would secure the building and streets around the arena for this event.

Just before the Russian nuclear blasts, the country was in a difficult state of affairs. Both political parties were as divided as ever in history. The recent unrest in the US caused some people to believe that law and order were going away. Radicals on both sides of politics actually became less abiding by law and order, and this caused a domino effect, causing lesser-known groups to take more radical approaches to get their message across. One group was comprised of Russian sympathizers living in the United States at the time, and they were planning to seize the Monument Center for their cause, which was to try to transfer the United States into an alliance with Russia and Russian-leaning countries. They were already camping in large numbers just outside of Rapid City.

This group was ultra-secretive about its movement, and Brad had no indication of this impending problem. Chris and the FBI didn't know of this group either. But the group knew of Terry and his transportation team, and they also knew of Chris and the FBI, of course. The Russian group had been testing the waters for a full-on assault on the Monument arena and the access to the Interstate between Rapid and Ellsworth. The Russian group wanted to take over the presidency and government during this weakened state of the union. They thought that they could seize the country by holding the president hostage and substituting their new president, who would eventually pardon them later. If this hostage mission failed, the backup mission would be to kill the president, and this mission came directly from the Russian Dictator through a complicated underground communication network.

The speech was to be at 6 PM local time, and the Russian sympathizers planned to act before the speech. All through the day, each of the separatists would sneak into the city and start his way toward the Monument Center. Each had a pistol and other weapons. By 2:00 PM, all forty or so separatists had made it to the Monument Center, and they were unnoticed because of the large group of people who wanted to hear firsthand what the president had to say.

At the same time, about seven separatists had snuck into a large culvert under Interstate 90 (I-90) that was between Ellsworth AFB and Rapid City. It was about halfway between these two places, in a rural setting. They placed explosives on the top inside of the concrete pipe and then hard-wired them to one another with one trigger mechanism and an antenna just outside of the pipe. With that complete, they left one at a time to avoid attracting attention and met up on a hillside just west of I-90. At this hillside location, they had a drone that was fully charged and had another switch that would set off the explosions when activated at 6:00 pm, the time that the president's speech was to start. The mission for these men was to blow up the interstate to eliminate military personnel from getting to the Monument Center quickly, and also to force the president to be flown back to the base if he was not taken hostage. These men were in radio contact with another person that was an observer in the crowd at Monument Center.

All of these men made it safely to the hillside and stayed out of sight and watched for the caravan of government vehicles, including the Beast, to pass by as they were going to the Monument Center. They didn't know when this would be, so they just waited.

Chris had his FBI personnel surrounding the Monument Center, which took a lot of people due to the size of this facility. At this time, Terry, Ryan, and Ann were with the Secret Service, waiting on the president and his wife. At about 4:00, everyone but Terry entered the Beast (the president's vehicle) and other heavily protected vehicles. Ann, Ryan, and the Secret Service were in the Beast with the president, his wife, and the Secretary of State. The convoy was off, with Terry and 15 other bikers in front and the back of the convoy. Highway patrol cruisers were also in the lead for traffic control. It took half an hour to get to the Monument Center, and the convoy drove into the facility, but Terry and his team stayed both inside and outside of this drivable entrance. Nobody suspected a thing until they heard building alarms indicating that someone was going through a locked entrance. All of Chris's team were on guard, but nothing happened for about 5 minutes, which gave all security Leads a chance to communicate. Nothing was happening except the alarm, which caused a full search of the facility by the FBI and Rapid City police department. As mentioned earlier, there are two large arenas in the complex, one for the indoor football league and one for the hockey team. Also, this facility had many convention-sized rooms and one area (the Barnett Fieldhouse) for even larger convention space. The president was to speak at the larger, newer Summit Arena, which seats more than 10,000 people.

The Monument personnel could not tell where the alarm came from, even though it was designed to show break-in locations, so this was confusing and uncomfortable. Chris was with the Monument security team at this point and asked if they had any false alarms in the past, but they didn't, so they silenced the alarms so as not to alarm the crowd any further.

Crowds of people were already entering the Summit Arena at this time because those doors were already unlocked and alarms were off, so streams of people were already filling the seats in the arena and this made things worse because they couldn't ask people to leave, or panic might break out. For this reason, Chris had many of his FBI team take up locations in hallways that separated the Summit Arena from the other parts of Monument Center. If someone had broken into another part of the Monument Center, they'd need to go through Chris's FBI team first. And if it was just some kid playing a joke, then they'd eventually find him later.

Ryan and the Secret Service let the president know of the situation at 5:45, and the president was fine with continuing the event. Fifteen minutes later, the president started to walk on stage when a large blast was heard east of town, just after the separatist drone was flown within signal of the explosives under Interstate 90. It was a large explosion, and all four lanes of the Interstate were destroyed, leaving a huge gap in the middle of the Interstate so no vehicles could pass.

Immediately, Ryan, Ann, and the Secret Service ran out to get the president off stage. This blast was the signal for the separatists to start the assault from two directions: one from the hallways where the FBI was protecting between the Summit Arena and the remaining areas on Monument Center, and the second assault was on Terry and his biker team waiting at the vehicle entrance to the arena.

The FBI was outgunned, and it's still a mystery as to how the separatists entered the building with so many weapons. Chris and many of his FBI team were either injured or killed. Chris was grazed by a bullet but not bad enough that he didn't return fire as the separatists charged into Summit Arena. People were screaming and in complete panic, and this was exactly what the Russians wanted. They knew any security would not fire into a crowd.

On the other end of the facility, Terry's guys were under attack, but they were a little more street-smart and had immediately looked for cover and vantage point as soon as the explosion was heard. Also, even though they were not supposed to have automatic weapons, many of them did, so when the separatists came after them, the separatists found themselves outgunned. But that didn't stop a huge gunfight in this area of the parking lot. The separatists outnumbered Terry's team and were winning this fight.

Terry radioed Ryan and learned that Ryan, Ann, and the Secret Service had both the president and his wife just off stage and that many separatists were running towards them now through the crowd. With few options, Terry told them to get the Beast started, and they did.

At this point, the separatists had the advantage, and that's when Ryan had an idea and coordinated it with Terry. A couple of minutes later, fifteen of Terry's team, as well as himself, started their Harleys up in a loud fashion. Then Ryan, driving the Beast, lunged forward and out of the arena, followed by sixteen Harleys waiting inside and outside the vehicle entrance. The separatists turned their attention on the Beast and blasted it with everything they had as it made it to North Fifth Street, turning left to North Street, while the sixteen Harleys quickly turned right and less noticed.

The Beast was a well-fortified vehicle but had a tough time making it much further than a block north on North Fifth Street while the separatists ran after it and overtook it near North Street. They surrounded it and opened the doors. The only person in the vehicle was Ryan and this was confusing as the separatists needed the president as a hostage to keep themselves safe. Now, they were just sitting ducks with the Rapid City Police Department surrounding them. One separatist tried to grab Ryan, but he blasted him with his pistol, and the other separatists ran for cover at nearby homes in this north Rapid City neighborhood. But the neighbors weren't having it. Several homeowners shot at them through windows and doorways, and this caused the separatists to scramble around. It didn't take long for the Rapid City police to capture the remaining separatists.

Other separatists who ran through the arena towards the stage finally made it to where the Beast was, but it was gone. They ran out in the street, only to see their comrades being arrested on North Street, and that's when Chris and other surviving FBI agents came up behind them. It was over for them, and they knew it, so they surrendered easily.

The crowd from the arena settled a little once the shooting stopped, and there was confusion everywhere, but things were safer now.

Chris went up to North Street, where the Beast was stopped, and found Ryan getting out of the vehicle. This was even more confusing until Ryan told Chris that he and he alone drove the Beast out of the arena. Chris was glad to hear this, but the natural question was, where are the president and his wife? Ryan said he'd show him, and the two got into a police car and drove downtown, where in front of the Firehouse Restaurant were sixteen Harleys.

Note: The Firehouse winery is a part of the Firehouse restaurant, which has its vineyard as a neighbor to the AC-DC-AC station in Rapid City. The winery's Facebook page has a picture of the station in the background.

Ryan, Chris, and the driver of the police car walk in, only to find the president and his wife, along with Anne, drinking beers (Spearfish IPA's). The Secret Service was there also, but they were not drinking anything. The patrons in the restaurant were all in awe of the situation, and a few minutes later, Chris had the place completely secured with the FBI, Rapid City Police, and just about every other security team around them, including other Secret Service agents. Then, the president said something that nobody expected. He said let's go back to the Summit arena and finish this thing, and that's what they did.

Concurrent with this, the wounded FBI agents and members of Terry's Team were being treated for injuries, and the Russian sympathizers were being loaded into police vehicles.

The crowds were settling down inside and outside of Monument Center and knew that the bad guys were dead or arrested. Then they heard the loud sound of bikers driving up North Fifth Street, and they turned back into one of the main entrances to the Summit Arena and parked there. To the shock of bystanders, the president got off the back of one Harley, and his wife got off the back seat of another. A couple of Secret Service agents were also on Harleys, but most of them were in a separate vehicle close by. They were met by many of Terry's team for protection, but the president wanted people to see that he was okay and that he was going to give the speech one way or the other. The news traveled fast, and the crowds came back into the arena. Chris returned there and was helping his wounded FBI agents into an ambulance, but rather than go to the hospital himself, he joined the Secret Service, Anne, Ryan, and Terry, and they all escorted the president and his wife.

The crowd was shocked to see the president on a Harley and even more surprised to see him escorted by people who were themselves injured, but these are not normal times, and the country must go on. The truth is that the president requested the ride on the Harley back to Monument Center. He wanted to show strength to the bystanders.

The speech from the president is shown below, and it was all ad-libbed.

"Good afternoon, and thanks for coming back into this beautiful Summit Arena. Today, we in Rapid City have all witnessed Russian Sympathizers trying to take over our government. But thanks to brave teams of security personnel, they were not successful. The wounded from this assault are being treated now and will be taken to the Monument Health Hospital. We don't know the full extent of the injuries or, God forbid, fatalities, but we do know that America is stronger than ever thanks to their sacrifices.

To those listening to this on radio, an unsuccessful attempt to take me and my wife hostage has failed, and we are in full control. Our government is as strong as ever. You will be updated on this situation as we learn more about what happened, but for now, we need to let the law enforcement and hospital staff do their jobs.

My speech today was to encourage and update you on the progress of communications within the damaged areas of the United States. We have made significant progress in this third week after the blast and anticipate having 70 percent of the country back with power by the end of next week, the fourth week after this unprovoked attack from Russia. I'd like to thank all of those who have made this a reality, and I'll say it happened at a much faster pace than I could have imagined. It shows the spirit of the American people, and it also shows the kindness and dedication of our neighboring countries as well as those overseas.

In the weeks that follow, our supply chain will be moving again. It will take months to get back to where we were before the blast, but you can be assured it will happen.

As I mentioned in my first speech, it is my obligation to tell you the full truth, and that is that some parts of our power grid will take many months to repair. The reason is that the very largest of transformers take time to build, but they have been started. In the interim, some level of power will be restored to the vast majority of the country.

Given that power is coming back, other utilities will be online after that.

The security in most of the areas of the country is at acceptable levels, but I ask that you remain vigilant and prepared to help one another as needed.

I will leave you now with these final words: We Will Survive this because America Can Not Be Defeated. Thanks, everyone, and God Bless America as well as our Neighbors and Allies".

After the speech, the president turned to Chris and thanked him for standing while injured. Then, he waved over some medical staff to help him off to the hospital. Chris's injury was not bad because the bullet just grazed the fleshy part of his leg. It bled some making it look worse than it was, and it certainly didn't stop him from performing his job with all the adrenaline surging through his veins.

The Interstate was not passable, so a military helicopter, previously waiting at a parking lot near Monument Center, was dispatched to pick him up. This helicopter was for emergency situations. Ryan and Ann both got in with the president and his wife, along with the Secret Service and then they took off for the trip back to the Base.

At this same time, Brad had been with eight of his hired patrol guards on Interstate 90, trying to figure out how the separatists were able to blow up both lanes of the Interstate. They had been searching since the interstate blast and could see tracks going up to the hillside west of I-90 (east of the Rapid Valley area). It was a big area, given the miles of land between Rapid City and Ellsworth AFB, but they were going to search every hiding place.

When Brad heard that a helicopter was to transport the president back to the Base, he requested some more time to check out the hillside in an attempt to find those responsible for blowing up the Interstate. The Base responded that they would hold back for 10 minutes, but that was not enough time for Brad and the eight guards that were with him.

Brad and the guards had followed the tracks and bent grasses for a couple of miles and started to smell what appeared to be tobacco. It was faint but real, so they split up into groups and cautiously continued.

The separatists were bored, given the time since the blast, and many of them were almost sleeping when they noticed Brad and the other guards. One separatist was so startled he haphazardly took a shot with his pistol, even though he was too far for the shot. This shot was fortunate because it gave away their location. Everyone then took cover, and a gunfight was underway.

Brad immediately called the Base Security and told them to ground the helicopter, but they refused, so the helicopter took off for the Base. The Base didn't think the gunfight could affect the helicopter if it flew high enough over the Interstate. It was flown by a Viet Nam-era pilot from Lusk, Wyoming.

The separatists' mission was twofold. The first part was completed by blowing up the Interstate. The second part was just about to unfold, and it was the main reason that they had seven people with them: protection in case they were spotted, just like what was happening now. Five of them had automatic weapons to protect two individuals who operated a portable antiaircraft weapon to kill the president if he survived the hostage attempt. When the separatists were spotted, the two with the antiaircraft weapons quickly moved away from the group and expected the other five separatists to protect them.

The gunfire was tremendous, and Brad and his guards had to retreat to find cover. It was very strange as to why the separatists didn't simply leave once the Interstate was blown up? Brad asked the guards to hold the line while he snuck up the hill more in an attempt to flank the separatist. When he got to the top of the hill, he could see and hear the helicopter getting closer as it followed the Interstate toward the Base. Then he saw two separatists preparing to fire the antiaircraft weapon, which Brad recognized immediately. Brad had no time to contact the helicopter because the separatists were within moments of firing the weapon. Brad had to act fast as he steadied his Colt 45 as best he could and then took a shot. He didn't hit either separatist, but he did hit the weapon just as it was being shot. Brad's shot forced the antiaircraft weapon to shoot low rather than towards the helicopter. The heat-seeking projectile sought out the nearest heat source, which happened to be a BBQ grill that the guards used to cook food. The charcoals were still hot in the BBQ, so this was blown to smithereens.

The percussion from this blast knocked the helicopter a few feet, but the experienced pilot easily got it under control, flew out east further, and then safely returned to the Base.

The separatists knew that their mission was very risky, but they didn't expect what would happen next. The Army National Guard was immediately mobilized from the Rapid City airport and came flying over the hill from the west (Rapid City Regional Airport) in full force with two Black Hawk helicopters, all ready for assault. They were ready, willing, and hoping to transport the president, but Ellsworth AFB chose to use its own helicopter that was previously placed at Monument Center for emergencies. In any case, they were ready and easily overcame the separatists.

Brad and the guards went back to normal duties, and all the living separatists were taken to detention sites on Base for questioning.

These gunfights cost the lives of 3 FBI agents, and 27 Russian separatists. All of the Americans that died were given the Presidential Medal of Freedom in a subsequent televised ceremony after power was restored.

MONUMENT CIVIC CENTER

Rapid City, South Dakota

CHAPTER 13 – RUSSIAN GOVERNMENT COLLAPSE

The collapse of the Russian government was so fast it was shocking even to the United States government. It seems that the HEMP effort from Russia was a last-straw attempt to supercharge their military and economy. The long war in Ukraine, as well as the attempt to mask the damages of being isolated from much of the world, had taken a huge toll. Russia did a good job in masking their problems, but after their failed attempt to cripple the United States military, it was a lost battle to try to mask anything anymore.

The Russian Dictator and his circle of people vanished. Airplanes constantly took off from Moscow for hours on end, and they were tracked to many countries around the world, but the United States could not tell who was aboard. Also, ships and large boats were leaving from every port in Russia.

It remains unknown why Russia (and North Korea) didn't use nuclear weapons other than on the HEPM missiles. The best answer is that the leaders wanted to escape somewhere else if they were unsuccessful, and no country would accept them if they did. It is also possible that they knew it would be the death of the Russian population at a much greater scale.

Conventional missiles destroyed all of the Russian Dictator's homes, so the United States didn't know if he was dead or alive. However, the United States military kept track of all planes and boats and eventually caught up with many from the Russian Dictator's inner circle. They were all arrested and would eventually be tried, just like the Nuremberg Trials. Hanging would be the preferred way of execution, just like after World War II.

The people of Russia were on their own. The military and government had no plans to help the civilian population. Everything and all money went into the military and government operations. It was like they didn't care about the real Russian people. As in the United States, the rural population was more prepared for survival than the cities. Similar problems existed in Russia after its defeat, but no help would come for the Russian people until many months after the blasts occurred. Ironically, the first help came a few months after the blasts from NATO countries in the form of airdrops to several large cities, including Moscow.

The future government for the land mass that was Russia before the blasts struggled to take place. In the interim, the nuclear sites that still existed were protected by contract personnel who were part of the Russian military. Funds for these people came from many countries, and monitoring of the protection came from NATO countries and satellite observation from the United States Space Force.

The Russian economy was in shambles. Bartering became one way to gain food or supplies, and for a while, the Russian Rubel remained accepted in some areas deep in the country. However, as communication became more available, the Rubel lost its value, and other currencies from stable economies, including the dollar, were used. Needless to say, millions of people died within the first year after the blasts, and most of them were in cities. Eventually, armed trucks would appear in many locations to sell food and goods, but only for acceptable currencies in nearby countries, such as the Euro and the Dollar.

Unfortunately, no free country would invest in Russia, thanks to the Russian Dictator. His dream of rebuilding the old USSR into a strong world power had done the opposite, and it was the people of Russia who paid the price of allowing their Dictator to destroy their country.

Ruthless groups of people tried to gain control of the government, and there was a lot of civil war-type fighting.

CHAPTER 14 – THE WORLD TAKES A SHORT BREATH

This disaster was almost over, and the world was once again safe from worldwide conflict, at least for now. All countries on the globe learned from this conflict. The larger countries took precautions to harden their critical power grids and other electronic equipment. But it wasn't just electronics that were hardened. The world population has also been hardened towards dictators who think it's okay to make empty threats with nuclear weapons. It's always been a rough world and always will be. These modern times are no exception.

The advent of nuclear weapons in the 1940s set up a new world order, where an attack on a country that had nuclear weapons would mean destruction from a counterattack. The HEMP attack was an attempt by Russia to eliminate any counterattack, but that didn't work at all, and Russia bore the brunt of destruction from this conflict.

Technology will always be used for both good and bad, and both need to be expected and planned for. Dictators will always want to expand their reach to previous tribal boundaries, such as Hitler's Third Reich or the Russian Dictator's land grab attempt in Ukraine, but history has proved that this will eventually lead to failure and the suffering of millions of innocent people.

CHAPTER 15 – REBUILD BUT THIS TIME BETTER

If there was a larger human-made being other than the power grid, it would be the United States economy and associated supply chain. In the history of the United States, there has never been an absolute stop to the economy and supply chain so this was a first, but most people had some taste of it during and after the COVID-19 pandemic and how the supply chain was resolved after that event.

It's obvious that the supply chain is worldwide now, and this was to the benefit of the United States. Most other economies in the world were not broken like the United States, and it was these economies that helped repair the US supply chain fast.

It was not just the power grid that was to be rebuilt better. The federal government was looking for an overhaul due to the political unrest between both political parties that didn't seem to have a reasonable off-ramp. In addition, having the president in charge of so many non-defense issues didn't make sense as problems became more complicated. For the important issues, Congress was actively looking at revising the executive branch of the government. It would need to be a major change in the constitution, but most people in both parties were sick of the constant head-banging with each other. The changes were considered basic to the security of the United

States, giving more power to the voting public. Here are the main points...

The president would continue the specific role of defense of the Country and the people of the United States and this would include these three cabinet offices: state, defense, and homeland security, and be tied to the constitution and maintaining a true democracy. However, many cabinet offices within the current government structure would be separated from the president's management and become independent agencies but still a part of the executive branch of the government.

The Current cabinet departments with proposed changes

State – to remain under the presidency

Treasury – not under the presidency and voted on by the public

Defense – to remain under the presidency

Attorney General – not under the presidency and voted on by the public

 Interior – not under the presidency and voted on by the public

 Agriculture – not under the presidency and voted on by the public

 Commerce – not under the presidency and voted on by the public

Labor – not under the presidency and voted on by the public

Health and Human Services – not under the presidency and voted on by the public

Housing and Urban Development – not under the presidency and voted on by the public

Transportation – not under the presidency and voted on by the public

Energy – not under the presidency and voted on by the public

Education – not under the presidency and voted on by the public

Veterans Affairs – not under the presidency and voted on by the public

Homeland Security – to remain under the presidency

There were two main reasons for these changes suggested above.

1. This clearly provided the president with one main obligation: protecting the people of the United States, the Constitution, and a free democracy. In recent years, it became clear that many people vote primarily due to one or more specific issue other than those that relate to the Departments of State, Defense, and Homeland Security. Securing our Country and our democracy are primary.

2. The voters would decide the remaining cabinet offices and could be from either political party, splitting up these serious issues of the Country from the election of a president.

Control of the government would once again go to the American voters, at least as much as possible with a democracy.

The hardest part of this HEMP attack was over. Now, it was time to repair or rebuild. The Country, in general, was improving fast. Of course, some areas were more difficult due to population density and proximity to where the nuclear blasts occurred. Areas of the Country rebuild at different paces, such as......

New York and large population areas of the eastern seaboard: When power was restored on the eastern seaboard, the cleanup was swift. The subway system was dried out, and trains were replaced as best as possible, given that every engine was unworkable due to water damage. Any structural damage was repaired immediately, and each section of the track was tested and retested for functionality. At this same time, the street level was repaired to include power to street lighting and traffic signals. After that, vehicle traffic came back immediately.

The storm sewer drained well, and any obstructions were cleaned. The most difficult public utility was drinkable water. The entire system needed to be sanitized, so the utility warned the public not to drink water from this system for one week. In that week, the utility got the system pressurized and then sent higher-dosed chlorinated water through the system before going back to regular drinking water standards. Every section was finally tested, and then, after a week, the system was good to go again.

Officials from every part of government, from city to county, to state, to federal, were involved in the removal of the dead. The removal of the dead occurred everywhere, with the most occurring in homes and high-rises. Every day for a week straight, you could see emergency vehicles traveling to mass morgues. Every community had them, but the densely urban areas were the worst. Eventually, the stench of death gave way to what life was before the Russian blasts.

Not everyone could afford to have their deceased loved ones dug up and reburied. It was for this reason that the original burial sites became permanent graveyards. Many were in parks or open spaces in the city, and these new grave sites eventually became constant reminders of this HEMP war.

Chicago and the Midwest to Oklahoma: In this large Midwest area, the larger populated cities experienced very similar rebuilding to the eastern seaboard, but outside the populated cities, it was much better. Fortunately, the weather was excellent during this time of year, and you could actually see happiness as neighbors helped neighbors. The Midwest was truly the American dream for rebuilding after the blasts.

Denver and the Front Range from Cheyenne, Wyoming to Pueblo, Colorado PLUS Salt Lake City, Utah from Ogden to Provo: The first thing that the governors of both Colorado and Utah did was to get the National Guard out to clear up gang activity in the larger cities. Fortunately, this didn't take long, and the cleanup was swift. Most of the dead were found in high-rise neighborhoods, where food and water were more difficult to get. The suburban areas of the Front Range of Colorado and the populated areas of the Salt Lake City area were reasonably well off. Most deaths in these areas, as well as rural areas, came from neighbor disputes. As with most of the Country, the rural areas were much more prepared for emergencies like this, and these areas returned to normal fast.

Minneapolis and Saint Paul Metropolitan Area: Minnesota and the lake region of South Dakota are mentioned separately from other midwestern areas because of the uniqueness of the many lakes that were left after the last ice age. These lakes helped this area greatly with fresh water and food, saving many lives. Unfortunately, the inner-city areas had it worse here, and it was much more difficult to get back to normal. Like Chicago and New York, the large downtown neighborhood had the most deaths and suffering.

Here, the rural areas were much better off than the cities. The land is rich for farming, and the blasts occurred at harvest time, so food was also more available in the form of vegetables and different fruits. Generally speaking, this area recovered faster than most.

Florida and Southern States: It was greatly beneficial to have the coast lined on three sides of this state, making it unique. If the population were smaller, Florida would have come out of this emergency faster. Many large cities experienced problems in high-rise neighborhoods, and many people were just not prepared for the supply chain to be out for weeks. The citrus crop is typically in January, so the fruit was green at the time of the blasts, but other crops were in season, and of course, the sea fishing helped feed many during this emergency period. In general terms, Florida came back to normal quickly.

Texas - Dallas, Fort Worth, Houston, Austin, San Antonio: The Texas grid came back before the western and eastern grids and happened because of the northern location of the nuclear blasts. This news was a pleasant surprise for the federal government since so much military is located in San Antonio. The AC-DC-AC substations were disconnected from the western and eastern grids until all grid systems were back online.

The large cities in Texas experienced problems similar to those in Denver, Colorado, except in the coastal areas. Water was less available in West Texas due to the dryer climate, but rain did fall and saved many lives.

Texas took care of Texas, and the survival rate was better here due to a more prepared population.

The rural areas in Texas survived much better than the cities. Generally speaking, the rural folks are independent people and don't rely on others very much. This independence is true for both ranchers and farmers, but many of these folks traded food items, such as meats, for vegetables or fruits. Many had their own fuel supplies for equipment on ranches and farms, so they were able to get around more than most. All of them had guns for protection and hunting, and most looked out for their neighbors. Outsiders dare not trespass, or they will put their lives on the line. Communication and healthcare were the two main issues in the rural areas.

Phoenix and Tucson: The desert southwest was the second-to-worst place to be after Southern California. Water and heat issues were the main issues, and many deaths here were more attributed to lack of water than lack of food. If there was one advantage in Arizona it was the proximity to Mexico. Mexico was much less impacted by the blasts, so aid from Mexico came quicker in the form of water, food, and fuel.

The areas higher in elevation survived better because it was cooler and had more rainfall. The Flagstaff area was the best place to be for survival. The Lake Havasu area was also a better place to be during this time, even though it was hot, due to the large freshwater lake and river nearby.

Los Angeles and Southern California: Southern California was in shambles after weeks of the supply chain down. The saving grace for this area was the shipping lanes from other countries. Of course, power (electricity and fuel) was needed to crane supplies off the ships, so this became the priority. But that didn't save many on the coast from the extremely large influx of desperate people going coastal from the hot inland portions of the area.

The residents of the downtown high-rise area were somewhat trapped because surrounding areas became battlegrounds for food and water. These high-rises, as well as the less prepared coastal population, experienced more deaths than anywhere else.

San Diego fared better because it was so close to supplies from Mexico, but the area between Los Angeles and the Bay Area survived the best.

Many people from LA made it as far as Santa Barbara on the 101, although it was a solid jam-up between Ventura and Carpinteria. At least one of the three lanes stayed open, but the other two were parking lots of vehicles that ran out of gas. If a vehicle stalled in the one free lane, it would be moved out of the road by following vehicles. Anyway, this was as far as people from LA went. The Hollister Ranch was unaffected, where the super-rich owned homes on many acres of land. Also, the Santa Ynez Valley was unaffected. People from the Bay Area didn't make it any further south on the 101 than King City and this meant that very few people made it to the area between Paso Robles and Santa Maria, including the coastal areas from Cayucos to the Five Cities (including Pismo Beach and Arroyo Grande). This area was one of the safest locations in the state, next to the far northern area of California.

Bay Area of California plus Sacramento, Stockton, and Tracy: As mentioned earlier, the bridges to and from the San Francisco Peninsula were closed to everyone except for emergencies and so this isolated the million or so people from the rest of the Bay Area and made it more survivable. The other parts of the Bay Area did better than most of the United States because of the fresh water in the delta as well as the food source from the sea and surrounding rivers (Sacramento River and San Joaquin River). In addition, this area is rich in farm-grown vegetables and fruits.

Gangs existed here in larger than average numbers, but people's desperation was less, so generally, this large populated area fared reasonably well. But it was not as good as the far north of the state, where the population is much, much lower.

The Northwest from Portland to Seattle: Water was a lesser problem in the Pacific Northwest, and the rural areas did much better here than much of the Country. Even the suburbs of both Portland and Seattle survived better than other areas in the western United States. However, the inner cities of both Portland and Seattle were not as lucky. The larger-than-normal homeless populations created a bigger need, and the high-rise residents added to this need. Most deaths occurred here due to starvation. Unfortunately, this area was in its hot time of year, so the garbage and sewage in most urban areas began to create disease, and many were sick just before power was restored. The CDC prioritized this area, and the disease infections were controlled quickly.

The good thing about the Pacific Northwest was that it was far from the blasts over California.

CHAPTER 16 – CONCLUSION

A couple of months after all cities gained control of the crime associated with the power grid going down, the president of the United States invited Brad (lineman), Jim (dispatch manager), and all of the people who worked in dispatch and the power companies that saved the grid in eastern Wyoming, western South Dakota, and the Nebraska panhandle. There were 36 people in all. In a nationally televised appreciation briefing, the president, the federal western power Administrator, and his Lead Manager were lined up to give an award to each person and shake their hand. Every one of the 36 people walked in a line up towards the president, and everyone shook the hand of the president and Administrator, but when the Lead Manager for the federal power administrator put out his hand, nobody shook it. Some would ignore him outright, and some (including Brad and other IBEW members) just stared at him in disgust as they walked by him. The president and everyone in the country noticed this, and a few months later, this Lead Manager was working a different job in an undisclosed location. He wasn't fired, but he was put in a position in which important decisions were not needed. The president then instructed the Department of Energy to ensure that anyone replacing the Lead Manager's job would have a hands-on power background, and linemen and other power technicians need to be considered for this job.

A Japanese company had perfected a hydrogen-fueled power generator that could generate power for individual houses. They also designed and developed a small wind turbine that could remove hydrogen from the air and supply it directly to the fuel bladder used by the hydrogen generator. Hydrogen is extremely flammable and could create explosions, but this Japanese firm had devised an ingenious way to keep this system safe. Households in Japan started to use this new product and connected them directly to the power grid, making the grid much safer. After the Japanese government worked out the payment details for the power companies and households that supplied the grid, the overall grid system became more stable and dependable because additional power generation was instantly available locally. Larger power plants didn't need to produce as much power to the grid anymore because the household hydrogen generation worked dependably any time of the day. The big power plants were still needed for commercial and overall system requirements, and they also continued to provide spinning reserves (potential power that can come online quickly with a simple switchgear connection).

Japan's amazing success with this new power grid system was immediately noticed worldwide, and the company that developed (and patented) the hydrogen generator with wind-supplied hydrogen was hit with so many orders that it couldn't keep up. This new technology changed the power supply everywhere, and all countries went in this direction. This technology was so successful that governments worldwide provided funds to buy out the patents from this Japanese company so that manufacturing plants could be constructed in every country. The developers of this technology were instantly billionaires.

The hardening of electronics has become a major industry worldwide. The early Faraday's cage design was dramatically improved and connection openings (for conductors and cabling) to these new cage designs were also made reliable for as high as gamma frequencies. Designing for a HEMP attack or solar flares became a normal part of design for critical infrastructure. Design for new vehicles also incorporated hardening components.

Millions of people died in both the United States and Russia from starvation, lack of water, or violence. The actual numbers will never be known, and deaths will continue to occur in Russia until a new government is formed and the economy returns to some degree of normal. It was the greed of the Russian Dictatorship that did this, and it will never be forgotten by the surviving Russian population and the entire world.

The lives of Brad and Ella changed for the good. Brad's boss wanted him to start training to take over his job after he retired. Brad thought about it and decided he didn't want the stress of his boss's job, and he didn't want to be tied to an office job. He could easily remain a lineman into his fifties, and then perhaps he'd look into another type of job, but for now, he was happy with his work. Also, he still dreamed that one day, the coal under his property would make him a millionaire, so this was his dream for the next few years anyway.

This dream wasn't that far off. A new, high-tech, coal-burning power plant was currently being proposed in western Kansas. This power plant would be connected to many large ponds for growing algae. The CO_2 from burning the coal would be captured and piped to the large ponds where it would be used to grow algae, and the algae would be used as a potential food source. It was a completely clean environmental process that would be as acceptable to nature as any other form of power generation (generalized process = sulfur free coal + heat → power generation (with mechanical removal of particulates) + CO_2 → algae growth using CO_2 + H_2O → food source + clean H_2O + clean air).

A few years after the successful demonstration of this new power plant, Brad and Ella were offered a ridiculous amount of money for the 100 acres that they owned, and they became millionaires. Brad built another garage attached to his Gillette home and furnished it with two new Harley Davidson motorcycles. Brad would ride his new bike to work nine months out of the year. Yes, Brad continued to work as a lineman.

Tim (Dispatch Manager for the federal power agency) was one of the main prospects for the Manager's job under the Administrator. Rumor has it that he is a shoo-in for the job.

Troy, TJ, and the other CB and Ham radio operators became near celebrities, given their help during the crisis. People from all over the world wanted to learn about their stories, and book deals are underway, too.

Terry (Brad's biker friend from Gillette) was offered a security job at the coal plant he was working at. The slowdown in coal usage forced the company to downscale, so they offered Terry the job to keep him with the company until coal usage improved. Terry's biker friends were also working at the coal plant and were offered free training by the governor for solar or wind power fields. None of them liked leaving the coal industry, but they could not turn down a good-paying job.

Ryan and Ann were both paid well for their time working for Chris and the FBI. They were already well off financially, so they donated all their income to the "1880 Train" in their hometown of Hill City, South Dakota.

Shortly after the president relocated back to Washington, DC, he met (via teleconference) with the South Dakota Governor and the Director of the South Dakota Bureau of Investigation (SDBI headquartered in Pierre, South Dakota). They decided to create a branch office of the SDBI in Rapid City, South Dakota. Then they called Chris into the meeting. Chris didn't know what was going on, so he was completely caught off guard when they offered him the job of Deputy Director of the SDBI. Chris immediately accepted and was happy to move from Denver back to his hometown of Rapid City. He had the perfect experience after working for the Rapid City Police Department, the Denver Police Department (as an Investigator), and with the FBI. His first point of business is to hire Maka and Chaiton as Lead Investigators. Rumor has it that he previously tried to get them on with the FBI in Denver, but they would not leave South Dakota.

Maka and Chaiton accepted the jobs of Lead Investigators for the SDBI. They were perfect for this type of work because they had police experience and spoke fluid Lakota and English. It is important to note that all reservations are independent, and one reservation may not accept someone from another reservation, but being Indian helped them get their foot in the door when it came to issues on reservations.

Chris, Maka, and Chaiton, along with two office managers, would take on half of the SDBI's workload, and most cases would be in western South

Dakota. Their future would bring exciting and dangerous cases, so much so that these cases could fill a series of novels, but those are for another time.

Just before the one-year anniversary of the Russian nuclear blasts, Brad and his old high school friends were on their annual camping trip along a beautiful Canadian lake in upper Saskatchewan. Several other camping groups joined them this year: one group from the Fort Peck Indian Reservation, another was Mr. Russell, who had radio pals from both Canada and the United States, and Chris showed up with Maka and Chaiton. A biker group also joined for a few days: Terry, his wife, and Ryan and Ann. Brad and Ella also drove in with a new camper. You see, some of the best friends are made from difficult situations, and they all got together for drinks and fish BBQs at the end of each successful fishing day of the camping trip. On the last night of this year's fishing trip, they all pulled out their favorite alcohol, and this year's theme was Canadian Whiskies. Brad naturally brought his favorite Kentucky bourbon, Woodward Reserve. As they cooked the fish filets, Brad and others looked up in the sky and saw a small meteor shower crossing the upper atmosphere. Brad thought it could be the remnants of an old asteroid cluster and thought about the legend of Wichapi & Hotah and their story of the asteroid storm in the 1800s. He then toasted the beautiful night sky. At that, everyone also joined in on the toast. After all, it was a night of celebration. The power grids were up again in the United States of America.

REFERENCES

Reference below is included for technical verification and clarification of HEMP potential damages.

Reference 1:

Normal High-Altitude Electromagnetic Pulse u(HEMP) Waveforms

Technical Report

Submitted By:

Applied Research Associates, Inc. (Jonathan Morrow-Jones)

5425 Hollister Avenue, Suite 220

Santa Barbara, CA   93111

January 2019

For: Defense Threat Deduction Agency/RD-NTE

Approved for public release

THEORY OF EARLY-TIME HEMP WAVEFORMS
The theory of high-altitude, fast electromagnetic pulse signal starts from the idea that an electromagnetic current from a nuclear detonation is produced due to the mostly-radial outward movement of recoil electrons from Compton scattering. In Compton scattering, a gamma-ray from the nuclear detonation "collides" with an electron. This interaction causes the gamma-ray to transfer energy

to the electron, and moves the electron in a different direction. The outward moving Compton recoil electrons are also turned as they cross the geomagnetic field lines. The net motion of the electrons is the outward motion (radial) from the detonation plus transverse components from turning in the geomagnetic field. As they traverse through air, these electrons continue to interact with the air, depositing energy into the air or ionizing air molecules, creating conductivity. The amplitude and waveform shape of the electromagnetic pulse are therefore the result of the competition between the creation of the electrical current, which generates the electromagnetic fields, and the creation of conductivity, which dampens electromagnetic fields.

Reference 2:

High-Altitude Electromagnetic Pulse Waveform Application Guide

Electronic Power Research Institute (EPRI)

CESER Technical Analysis Reports

Page 5 and 6k

July 2023

For:

U.S. Department of Energy

Office of Cybersecurity, Energy Security, and Emergency Response

Potential Impacts of HEMP E1 is a large amplitude pulse with frequency content in the 100's of MHz; thus, conductive objects like control cables and power lines behave as antennae and absorb the radio frequency (RF) energy of the pulse. In this manner, the incident E1 field couples to overhead lines, control cables and so on and generates conducted voltage and current transients which insult connected equipment. This is referred to as the conducted threat. The incident E1 field can also couple directly to equipment and induce voltages and current transients at the circuit board level which can also lead to device upset or damage. This is referred to as the radiated threat....

E3 induces low-frequency (quasi-dc) currents in transmission lines and bulk power system transformers that have grounded wye windings. The flow of these geomagnetically induced currents (GIC) in transformer windings can cause magnetic saturation of transformer cores, which causes the transformers to generate harmonic currents, absorb significant quantities of reactive power, and experience additional hotspot heating in windings and structural parts. Potential impacts of E3 on the electric power grid include voltage collapse (regional blackout), protective equipment misoperation due to harmonics, and transformer damage due to additional hotspot heating [3]. Additionally, certain sensitive power electronics-based loads, for example uninterruptible power supplies, may be prone to disruption or damage due to harmonic voltage distortion that is transferred from the transmission system to medium-voltage and low-voltage systems.

Reference 3:

Wikipedia - 3.22.2024

*A **nuclear electromagnetic pulse (nuclear EMP** or **NEMP)** is a burst of **electromagnetic radiation** created by a **nuclear explosion**. The resulting rapidly varying **electric** and **magnetic fields** may couple with electrical and electronic systems to produce damaging current and **voltage surges**. The specific characteristics of a particular nuclear EMP event vary according to a number of factors, the most important of which is the **altitude** of the detonation.*

*The term "electromagnetic pulse" generally excludes optical (infrared, visible, ultraviolet) and ionizing (such as X-ray and gamma radiation) ranges. In military terminology, a nuclear warhead detonated tens to hundreds of miles above the Earth's surface is known as a high-altitude electromagnetic pulse (HEMP) device. Effects of a HEMP device depend on factors including the altitude of the detonation, **energy yield**, **gamma ray** output, interactions with the **Earth's magnetic field** and **electromagnetic shielding** of targets.*

History: The fact that an electromagnetic pulse is produced by a nuclear explosion was known in the earliest days of nuclear weapons testing. The magnitude of the EMP and the significance of its effects were not immediately realized

*During the **first United States nuclear test** on 16 July 1945, electronic equipment was shielded because **Enrico Fermi** expected the electromagnetic pulse. The official technical history for that first nuclear test states, "All signal lines were completely shielded, in many cases doubly shielded. In spite of this many records were lost because of spurious **pickup** at the time of the explosion that paralyzed the recording equipment."[3] During **British nuclear testing** in 1952–53, instrumentation failures were attributed to "**radioflash**", which was their term for EMP.*

*The first openly reported observation of the unique aspects of high-altitude nuclear EMP occurred during the **helium balloon**-lofted Yucca nuclear test of the **Hardtack I** series on 28 April 1958. In that test, the electric field measurements from the 1.7 kiloton weapon exceeded the range to which the test instruments were adjusted and was estimated to be about five times the limits to which the oscilloscopes were set. The Yucca EMP was initially positive-going, whereas low-altitude bursts were negative-going pulses. Also, the **polarization** of the Yucca EMP signal was horizontal, whereas low-altitude nuclear EMP was vertically polarized. In spite of these many differences, the unique EMP results were dismissed as a possible **wave propagation** anomaly.*

*The **high-altitude nuclear tests** of 1962, as discussed below, confirmed the unique results of the Yucca high-altitude test and increased the awareness of high-altitude nuclear EMP beyond the original group of defense scientists. The larger scientific community became aware of the significance of the EMP problem after a three-article series on nuclear EMP* *was published in 1981 by **William J. Broad** in **Science**.*

Reference 4:

UNCLASSIFIED

Electromagnetic Pulse (EMP) Protection and Resilience Guidelines for Critical Infrastructure and Equipment.

February 5th, 2019

Version 2.2

Developed by the National Coordinating Center for Communications (NCC)

National Cybersecurity and Communications Integration Center

Arlington, Virginia

There are many other good references on this subject, and the associated physics for the effects of a HEMP blast will continue to be refined. For this reason, the physics for hardening electronics will also continue to be refined. It's just another example of the push and shove of technology, and the planning for both the good and bad that can come from it.

DEFINITIONS

1. Compton Scattering:

    Wikipedia 12.12.2023

    Compton scattering (or the Compton effect) is the **quantum** theory of high frequency **photons scattering** following an interaction with a **charged particle**, usually an electron. Specifically, when the photon hits electrons, it releases loosely bound electrons from the outer valence shells of atoms or molecules.

    The effect was discovered in 1923 by **Arthur Holly Compton** while researching the scattering of **X-rays** by light elements, and earned him the **Nobel Prize for Physics** in 1927. The Compton Effect significantly deviated from dominating classical theories, using both **special relativity** and quantum mechanics to explain the interaction between high frequency photons and charged particles.

2. Radiation Hardening

    Wikipedia 3.22.2024

    Radiation hardening is the process of making **electronic components** and circuits resistant to damage or malfunction caused by high levels of **ionizing radiation (particle radiation** and high-energy **electromagnetic**

radiation),[1] especially for environments in **outer space** (especially beyond the **low Earth orbit**), around **nuclear reactors** and **particle accelerators**, or during **nuclear accidents** or **nuclear warfare**.

Most **semiconductor electronic components** are susceptible to radiation damage, and radiation-hardened (rad-hard) components are based on their non-hardened equivalents, with some design and manufacturing variations that reduce the susceptibility to radiation damage. Due to the extensive development and testing required to produce a radiation-tolerant design of a **microelectronic** chip, the technology of radiation-hardened chips tends to lag behind the most recent developments.

Author of the other books:

Not Intended for Humankind: Warning....Too much science for most people.

SYNOPSIS:

This story takes place in 2022/2023. A man named Jim Zimberman and his wife, who was 40 years old, retired in Colorado just before the COVID-19 pandemic hit. Unfortunately, retirement becomes boring because of restricted travel, so Jim experiments with electromagnetic frequencies, which he has researched over the past ten years. He wanted to experiment with electromagnetic beams, like the LASER, but not necessarily in the visible range. In doing this, Jim creates an elaborate computer program using known physics equations and stumbles across an unknown frequency (actually three frequencies) within the Terahertz Gap of the electromagnetic spectrum. What he finds is astounding. It turns out that the frequencies he finds create massive heat radiation. Just before he gets any further with his experiment, tragedy strikes in downtown Denver, Colorado, during an unanticipated clash between two extreme political groups. Politics in 2022 is much worse than during the 2020 election, and ultra-extreme groups developed on both sides of politics, leaving the vast majority of Americans in the middle with little representation. After a time, Jim gathers himself, but with a sense of strong revenge due to the tragedy. Jim realizes that he might have a way to get revenge, and at the same time, he might be able to end the ultra-radical politics within the United States.

Afterlife in the Higgs Field:

SYNOPSIS:

Have you ever wished that you could communicate with someone who has died?

What would you do if you could communicate through a cryogenic mechanism and video camera connected directly to the computer that allowed you to communicate with someone that has passed?

A retired engineer and avid reader of modern physics named Bret Zimberman created such a device, and he was in for the shock of his life and his afterlife.

The book "**Afterlife in the Higgs Field**" is about an amateur physicist who experimented with a super cold environment to see what happens when sub-atomic quantum particles stop moving. He wondered if the Higgs Mechanism (briefly explained in the book) would reverse and what would happen to the 3-dimensional physical world we all live in. As a result, he set up a camera outside the super cold area and then watched from his computer screen. To his surprise, movement occurred, and over time, he learned that he was indeed looking within the Higgs Field (or an interim space between the 3-dimensional world and the Whole-One (Deity). He learned that he was allowed to witness the passing of the Sole of physical beings to what he termed the Whole-One.

Surviving Asteroid Storm Super Element 126: On
YouTube

SYNOPSIS:

After the Big Bang occurred, and after standard
elements precipitated out due to the high pressure and
temperature of star-building and explosions of
supernovas, an unusual element was created under
rare conditions. This Element is so rare that it's only
found on a few planets within our entire universe, and
one of those planets is planet Earth.

......fast forward billions of years into the future.....

Asteroids, billions of years old, come crashing down
on the Black Hills of South Dakota and into the
eastern prairie. A free Band of Lakota Indians
witnesses the most spectacular light show on Earth.
The light show lasted for hours while the Indian
people took cover for their lives.

......fast forward 100+ years......

Soil erosion over the past 100+ years has uncovered
many dark-rock outcrops on ranch land as well as on
the Pine Ridge Indian Reservation. The locals
accepted these dark-rocks as ordinary landscapes, but
one young Lakota Indian man became more curious,
and the results he found were literally from out of this
world.

News of the Super Element brought fortune hunters from all over the country, and they descended on the Black Hills just like the gold rush days of the late 1870s. A modern Wild West begins, but it also has the modern dangers of adversary countries and inquisitive billionaires looking for a profit in the next significant invention.

Who owns this Super Element, and who will protect it from being stolen? In a "David vs. Goliath" situation, this small community of ranchers and American Indians from the Reservation stand up to enormous opponents. With help from others in and around the Black Hills, they fight for what is theirs and for the national defense of their country.

The book titled "Surviving Asteroid Storm Super Element 126" began billions of years ago when the elements of the universe were created. This new Super Element traveled in a cluster of asteroids for billions of years until some crashed onto planet Earth. The story revolves around a strange dark-rock found in a poor rural area in South Dakota. The people of this community are strong, resourceful, and independent. They have survived harsh environmental conditions for all of their lives. Still, even they seek help when an astonishing material, found only in one area of our planet, attracts influential individuals and desperate countries. Help comes from a variety of odd sources, including bikers from the Sturgis Rally and an army of old pickup trucks.

Children's book titled **The Sort of Tumble Weed**: short book with graphics. On YouTube.

The Story of TUMBLE WEED (called Tumble for short)

Tumble was short and stocky and lived among the tall and thin grasses. He was lonely because he couldn't see others like him. What Tumble didn't know at that time was that he would soon soar with happiness and with many friends.

SYNOPSIS:

Have you ever seen anyone teased at school?

If so, you will like reading the book Tumble Weed to your children. Tumble Weed was teased and alone, among others that he didn't resemble, but Tumble was about to see how wonderful things can be when he finds others who accept him.

Ultimately, Tumble doesn't tease back but wishes all others could be with him as he fits in with his new friends.

The book titled "The Story of Tumble Weed" shows that there are many different sizes and shapes of kids and that they all have good qualities. This book is a natural children's story, and I'm surprised it wasn't written 100 years ago, although it's more appropriate for today's young people.

Children's book titled **Old Red Number 1**: Possibly dated because dog racing is reducing in the US. On YouTube.

SYNOPSIS:

Old Red Number 1 was a racing dog back in 1912. He was horribly mistreated by his owner, John Rotman, even though he won all of his races. Then, after a terrible accident that broke Red's leg, a group of young kids took him in and nursed him back to health. They also made a bet with John Rotman that Old Red would beat any racing dog he has.